THE WHITE SPARROW

THE WHITE SPARROW

Roy Brown

Abelard-Schuman

London

561836

© 1974 Roy Brown
First published 1974

ISBN 0 200 72191 7

Abelard-Schuman Limited
450 Edgware Road,
London W2
and
Kingswood House
Heath and Reach
Leighton Buzzard
Bedfordshire

Compton Printing Limited
Aylesbury

Chapter One

One mild, twilit evening a few weeks before Christmas, three figures made their way along a stretch of disused railway track not far from London's river.

At the rear was a boy called Sprog. On his shoulder he carried an old shoestring duffle bag. This contained all his possessions, apart from what he wore: faded jeans, a tattered anorak and plimsoles so full of holes that, to avoid the cuts and jabs of stones, he skipped and jumped from sleeper to sleeper. The verges on either side of the rusting tracks were high with tangled nettles, making good cover but impossible pathways.

Several yards ahead the Boy's passage along the sleepers was more agile than Sprog's, kangaroo-like and sometimes dishearteningly fast. At his heels, a small rough-haired mongrel, crippled in one hind leg, hobbled along the side of the track, sometimes pausing to raise the damaged limb and wet into the nettles.

Sprog, feeling he couldn't keep up this pace for much longer, wished that the Boy, out in the open, would not always move at the speed of sound. What was the hurry? For once, they were not dodging coppers or out-running some violated shopkeeper bent on capture and retribution.

Twilight deepened into darkness and the firepoints of stars held a hint of frost. Boys and dog had come across the waste-land, leaving behind yet another cosy, but all too temporary, hideout in a watchman's hut. A glimpse of fresh rooftops gave Sprog new hope that the Boy, as usual, would soon smell out their next refuge.

"Hey, mate," called Sprog, in his husky, confidential whispered shout. "When do we find some place to kip?"

The Boy simply hitched his haversack higher and kept moving. A couple of minutes later his eyes imitated the stars and twinkled over his shoulder at Sprog. The face was in shadow — the awful, blurred, feature-burnt face which, even in light, no longer held terror for Sprog. He thought no more of it now than he might of a slightly crooked nose or a smile with a missing tooth.

The Boy did not speak — he never spoke; but there was a suggestion of reassurance in his brief waiting on the track, waiting for Sprog to close the distance. A few yards further along he left the rails, took a rough narrow path through beaten-down weeds and loped into shadows cast by a tall building on one side of the forgotten railway.

It was quiet here but from farther away came sounds from the river: tugs chirping, winches grinding. A riveting machine clattered, a launch motor purred and a cargo boat nosed cautiously into a bend with snorting diesels. The Boy opened a door.

They were in a high, hollow building with a huge roof glass letting in a patch of pale night sky. Sprog had already guessed that the Boy knew of this place: his lope along the rusty rails had had a purpose. Once inside, after the briefest look round, the Boy settled at once as if into a familiar home, unfastening his haversack and unrolling the tartan blanket he always carried. The quietness was so intense that Sprog could hear his own breath and the scratch of vermin's claws.

Not a cheerful place! It stank, too, like the inside of a huge dustbin. Sprog had once hidden in a dustbin.

"Pongs a bit, don't it?" Sprog said, speaking his thoughts aloud. He didn't want the Boy to think he was being ungrateful so he added, "Not bad, though. I mean, it feels warm and dry and that. We stopping here long?"

He expected no answer and he got none. The dim shape of the Boy continued making up his bed. The dog limped off, wet into a corner and sniffed at smells. The worse the stink, the more beguiled its senses. The Boy's mutt would stake a claim in a cesspool.

Sprog screwed up his nose and spread his ground sheet on the hard floor at a private distance from the Boy's, then wound himself in his own blanket. The dog limped back, eventually, and curled itself up beside the Boy. Sprog tucked his hands behind his neck on the half empty duffle bag and gazed up into the unfamiliar gloom. The roof glass gave a faint view of hazy stars and sometimes the more powerful light of a river beacon would sweep across, as regularly as the second hand of a watch.

Sprog abandoned lingering thoughts of supper and wondered about breakfast. There were more of the faint, crunching sounds not far from his head — like something small eating matchsticks. Turning sideways, he saw a single red eye fixed on him in alien curiosity. A rat! Sprog closed his eyes. Never a boy to brood for long upon imagined terrors, he slept the draughty night through.

When he awoke it was dawn light and a fine rain fell gently on the roof glass. He was not surprised to find that the Boy and his dog had gone out — probably hours ago. He sat up stiffly and yawned. The Boy had not troubled to pack up his bed. That, and the coming of daylight, made it pretty certain he'd be back soon.

Sprog gave their latest home a look over. It was a gaunt shell of a place, gutted of floors and stairways. Warped timber walls were clad with cobwebs and devoid of windows. Bits of rusty machinery and broken barrels stood in odd corners and, near big double doors secured by a heavy beam on brackets, leaned a large, empty cart with iron wheels and shafts dipping into rubbish.

The part where they had made their beds was a recess shut off from the main floor by a rough wooden partition eight feet high. A small door led in and out of the recess — the door the Boy had pushed open the previous night.

They were both soaking wet when they came in. The Boy had a shapeless newspaper parcel under one arm and the dog had a bone in its mouth which it took off to a corner with a mean, secretive air. The Boy flung Sprog an orange.

"Ta, mate," said Sprog, catching it one-handed. "Where's me bacon and eggs then?"

The Boy didn't rise to that. He sat against the wooden partition with his back half turned to Sprog. He rarely gave Sprog a full daylight view of his disfigured face.

Sprog said to the back, "Not all that comfy here, is it? Still, we'll get a bit of gear together then we might as well hole up for a while." He added, half questioningly, "If you want, that is."

In a way, the Boy was in charge. Sprog had tagged along with *him*, not the other way around. It was what the Boy had wanted that morning some time ago on the towpath of the canal. "Cheerio, then," Sprog had said, "See you around, eh?" But the mutt had sat there, wanting Sprog, and Sprog remembered how the Boy's face had made new folds of scorched skin and tears had spilled from his eyes, the awful mouth shaping disappointment and hurt.

So Sprog had tagged along.

They stayed put, on and off. It rained incessantly for the first few days. The broad roof sprung leaks and it was impossible for the boys to keep dry. They dragged their bits of bedding from one spot to another, trying to dodge the drips, but wherever they went a fresh trickle of water from somewhere snaked along the filthy floor under their blankets and they awoke with some part of their bodies drenched, teeth chattering. Then they had to wring out their bedding and hang it on rusty nails, but the blankets and old sacks they found were still damp when they wrapped themselves up in them again.

The dog took to sleeping under the cart and Sprog and the Boy followed its example. The floor there was made of hard-packed, uneven cobbles. They rummaged round the warehouse and found some damp, mildewy boards to smooth it out. It was no use going out in the rain and searching soaked junk heaps for mattresses.

However hard it rained, the Boy and his dog always crept away at nightfall. They came back in the morning, looking half drowned. The Boy, however, was never empty handed — he was a marvel at raiding milk floats. The milk was all right and sometimes there was a reasonably dry packet of buns, but there was no way of cooking the eggs. The Boy simply broke them against the wall and swallowed them raw. Sprog's stomach turned over. He wasn't trying that!

While the Boy and his dog slept, Sprog had a lot of time on his hands. He made several excursions of his own, darting from shelter to shelter. The derelict warehouse stood alone and unvisited behind the abandoned railway. There was a path of sorts winding towards riverside buildings a quarter of a mile away. The path was now just an oozing track crossing a swamp-like wilderness of beaten down grass and undergrowth.

Sprog would negotiate the path in his bare feet, tucking his plimsoles and socks under the zip of his anorak. At the edge of the swamp he'd wipe his feet on the wet grass and put his plimsoles back on.

Then Sprog would find himself in a street packed with terraced houses and, on each corner, was a small shop. He went on the nick in his usual fashion, using his pert, honest gaze and a penny or two, if he had them, to buy some little thing across the counter while he stuffed his pockets and the front of his anorak with anything he could reach. Those shops had nothing much, though; only things like comics, packets of crisps, bars of chocolate and newspapers. Sprog didn't read the newspapers. He and the Boy used them under their clothes to keep out the damp — it was a trick Sprog had learned from a tramp long ago.

Once or twice Sprog paused at the end of the street, hearing the distant hum of traffic, feeling that he was standing at the edge of a gold mine. There would be better pickings in the town, but he wasn't going there in this wet. The big town would keep. Sprog hadn't a looking glass handy, but the shopkeepers' eyes were better than mirrors: the way they stared at Sprog with that twin, deadly gaze which was a mixture of curiosity and pity.

Sprog, who had begun life on a church doorstep, lived a while in a Children's Home, and then been farmed out to foster parents, made a point of never inviting pity. Pity and kindness came in all shapes and sizes: policemen, people sitting at desks in dusty rooms, people asking questions and telling Sprog that things were for his own good. People who watched over him and lined him up and made him do things too often, and too regularly, and at inconvenient times; such as brushing his teeth and combing his hair and washing his face. People who wanted to be called "Sir" and "Madam", or even "Uncle" and "Auntie" or "Mum" and "Dad" — stuffing a sweet in his mouth with one hand and opening a cage door with the other!

One afternoon, when Sprog got home, he wondered how much longer they were going to stay there — not that there was anywhere much else to go. The rain had begun to ease off a little. The Boy and his dog were asleep as usual and, although Sprog could have done with some conversation, he left them to it. Sprog glanced through his comics and nibbled nicked crisps and chocolate — they hadn't eaten a proper meal for a week.

At last the Boy awoke, his eyes at once wandering to the roof glass to see how dark it was. Sprog went and squatted beside him.

"Nice snooze?" he asked, giving him what was left of the crisps and chocolate. The Boy took them and filled his mouth. He had a slow mechanical way of eating, as if his teeth were blunt.

Sprog tried to feed the dog a piece of chocolate, but it would never take food from Sprog, only from the

Boy. As usual, the Boy's eyes held a gently teasing expression and he made a point of showing Sprog how to do it.

"Very clever," said Sprog, but there were other things on his mind, things that had been piling up all through the long, wet day. "I've been thinking. If we stop here much longer, we're going to catch pneumonia. You don't seem to mind the wet."

The Boy's glance back had its gently baffling lack of answer. Sprog went on, smiling, not meaning to needle the Boy. "What about some action, eh? It's all right for you and your mutt. I bet you spend all night raiding coffee stalls and kipping down in boiler rooms. Well, it's time *I* got organized an' all. I'm going down the town tomorrow. I'm going to lift so much stuff they'll think I'm a furniture van. I've had enough of living like a bleeding fish in a puddle."

Having said that, Sprog felt all right again. All right about the Boy, even all right about the wet.

There was nothing much left to eat and his torch battery had run out long ago, so Sprog decided to kip down early. Listening to the rain on the roof he fell asleep with rosy thoughts of a better tomorrow.

Some time later he was aware of a shadow brushing against his face — as substantial as a cobweb — and the recess door opened giving the Boy and his dog their access to the night.

Chapter Two

A town absorbed Sprog as a river receives a drop of rain. That damp, straw-coloured head and slight, quick body blended at once into rain-swept streets and squelchy parks. If he had lost a little of his old independence since tagging along with the Boy, he soon recovered the knack of living on his wits — arts which he had learned in several months of running loose.

He was a fox with the cunning to outwit, a flushed partridge, a rabbit darting underground, a cat upon a wall. Sprog was a man of many parts: a tall five-year-old, or a short boy of fourteen; a cub at a barbecue, a child on a school outing, a football supporter proudly displaying a stolen rosette. Sprog knew when to run and when to stand still; when to stare and when to look away; when to hide and when to disclose himself.

On the whole he sought no company. He joined no street game, got involved in no escapade; yet he knew when to melt into a playground; when to feed ducks at a pond; when to speak up and when to remain silent; when to tell lies and when to speak the truth.

Sprog could readily assume the disarming smile or the frightened air of a lost child. He was the beguiling little tearaway with the seat out of his pants. He was the big brother, he was the little brother; the bold boy who hitched a ride in a truck, or the shy boy buying a gift for his Gran. Sprog would ask a policeman the time or chat up a milkman and deliver his bottles — or give out the hymn books at Sunday School.

Sprog was Sprog, but he could also be anybody he liked, any sort of kid others expected him to be. It was a gift.

One afternoon Sprog wandered into a jumble sale. He was late, but still in time to lose himself in a crowd of snatchers and bargain hunters. It cost 2p to get into the church hall. Sprog wasn't wasting 2p so he squeezed unobtrusively past a girl selling tickets and found himself in an Aladdin's cave of shoddy treasures. Tired harassed ladies were disposing of left-overs and for 3p Sprog bought two almost-pairs of wellingtons. Then, because nobody seemed inclined to stop him, he helped himself to a couple of torn macintoshes strewn on a pile of unwanted clothes.

Sprog carried the lot back to the warehouse. The Boy hadn't finished his sleep, but Sprog couldn't wait. He woke him up cheerfully by slinging a nearly-pair of wellingtons and one of the macs on his bed.

"Look what I got," said Sprog.

The Boy turned one white eye on them then closed it. Sprog went on, "Been to a jumble sale. You'd be surprised what they chuck out at them places. If I'd had a bit of cash I'd have got there early and bought a shopful of stuff. I nearly nicked a nice sofa, only there was somebody sitting on it."

The Boy opened his eyes again. It was hard to tell how much he understood of Sprog's chatter, especially his jokes. But he took some interest in the wellingtons and mac and tried them on.

"Would you believe it?" said Sprog. "It's stopped raining now. Sky was blue as I come in, but there's a nip in the air and I bet it's going to snow. We'll have to nick a sledge next, or a pair of skates apiece. Not that I lifted that lot, mind." Sprog was suddenly serious, as if he was saying something important. He dug a packet of biscuits out of the front of his anorak.

"I nicked these, though. You got to live, as the man said. And I've been thinking. We're always wanting something, aren't we?" He gave the Boy a sharp, enquiring look as though he had noticed something new about him. "You never seem to want much . . . but I could write a list a yard long." The Boy's eyes held a glitter which was hard to read, but which might have been some kind of comment.

Sprog munched another biscuit, the dog licking up the crumbs. "What I mean is, we've got to get organized. That's what I mean. Nobody gives us much, do they? So we got to nick it, or we got to get money. Takes a bit of thinking out, don't it?"

Sprog fell asleep that night without thinking anything much, yet, in the morning, there was an idea waiting for him — like an egg on a plate.

The roof glass had a pale, blue tinge like thick ice. The Boy came in with his arms full of frosty cartons of milk, eggs and a packet of cheese. He put this lot down and opened his anorak. There was a bundle inside which turned out to be a tightly rolled, very smart pair of gent's pyjamas — dark blue with red stripes. Also in the bundle were two pairs of socks. The bundle was slightly stiff and damp and the socks were turned inside out. There was a clothes peg trapped in one sleeve of the pyjama jacket, so Sprog didn't need to ask questions!

The Boy threw Sprog the bundle and Sprog said, "For me? Ta. You never come across a hot water bottle by any chance?"

Sprog drank milk and nibbled some cheese. He felt in more of a hurry than usual. He slipped on the mac he had scrounged at the jumble sale, then the wellingtons which were not quite a pair, nor quite a fit. His small feet slopped in them a little as he let himself out and plodded stickily along the path.

When he reached the street he called at the newsagent's shop — the one from which he'd stolen comics, chocolates and newspapers. A round-shouldered old man with a crinkled face, tired eyes and black thumbs was counting out newspapers. He didn't seem to notice Sprog at first, perhaps because Sprog's head scarcely showed above the tops of the piles. Some time went by and the newsagent didn't ask Sprog what he wanted, so Sprog told him: "Thought you might want an extra roundsboy."

The newsagent's eyes were not entirely discouraging. He pinned Sprog with a look over his half-moon spectacles.

"A bit young aren't you, sonny?"

"Not really," said Sprog. "You don't want to take no notice of me size."

The old man seemed to be counting the lines on Sprog's face. Sprog was ready to tell him a story which had worked before, in various emergencies, about his mother being a widow and having eight children to bring up — all younger than Sprog.

"Have you got a bike?" asked the newsagent.

Sprog had had the idea that bicycles were dished out with the job. "I expect I could get one," said Sprog.

Fortunately, the old man did not ask Sprog where.

"You must have a bike," he said. "Where do you

live?"

"Just round the corner," said Sprog.

"I haven't seen you about before."

That was an advantage! Sprog said, "We only moved in a few weeks ago — me dad works at the docks." Sprog had forgotten the story about his mother being a widow.

"Hmm," said the newsagent. He went on writing big numbers on the corners of newspapers while he made up his mind. "I may be short of a roundsboy this morning. Young Terry Hobson had a bad cold yesterday. Do you know Terry?"

Sprog looked straight back at the half-moon glasses. "I know his sister. She's in my class at school."

"I didn't know he had a sister," said the newsagent, smiling. "A young man for the ladies, are you?"

The shop door opened and two children came in. Sprog had a glimpse of gleaming bicycles propped up at the kerb outside. They were a girl and a boy, both a good deal bigger than Sprog. They gave Sprog a thorough look over, starting with his face, then letting their eyes drop slowly down to his odd wellingtons, then up again to his face, counting the missing buttons on his mac.

Sprog stood by the comic rack, keeping his hands in his pockets, minding his own business. For a long time there was a lot of coming and going; the rustle of papers being shoved into satchels, back chat, more kids propping bicycles outside, more stares — and, apparently, no Terry Hobson.

"So you've got yourself a job," beamed the newsagent when they'd all gone. "What did you say your name was?"

"I never," grinned Sprog. "It's Sprog."

"All right, Sprog. It won't be regular, mind. You can do some of the nearest streets, so you won't need a bicycle. Let me see . . . " He sorted out some newspapers, placing them in a satchel. "Parker Street, Mulberry Street and . . . oh yes, the flats in Benson Close. You know where they are?"

"Yeah," said Sprog. They were in Bangkok for all Sprog knew, but he'd find them.

"Off you go, then," said the newsagent. "Fold the papers neatly and mind they don't tear when you push them through the letter boxes. Some of them have magazines inside. Don't lose them, or get them muddled up. Bring the satchel straight back afterwards, then you'll get paid."

"How much?" said Sprog.

"One morning's work as relief roundsboy? Hmm, I think ten pence would be reasonable, don't you?"

"Sure," said Sprog. "Ta."

Back at the warehouse that afternoon Sprog couldn't wait for the Boy to stir, so he gave him a shake a bit early. "It's getting late," said Sprog. "It'll be dark soon. I thought you'd want to be off."

The mutt gave Sprog a resentful glare from the sack between the beds. The Boy sat up, immediately alert as usual, his eyes flicking over the warehouse. Sprog fished out his wages – all in one penny pieces.

"We're in business, mate." He counted out five coins on the Boy's blanket. "Got a job this morning – roundsboy, delivering papers. I'm only a relief, at the moment, but it might turn out to be steady. Decent old geezer at the shop." Sprog took on a pensive look.

"Could do with a bike on that job, really. The other kids have all got bikes. Still, I've got to go back tomorrow. I did a good fast job so I might get a bigger round. We'll be rolling in it soon, mate — rolling."

But the Boy didn't touch the coins on his blanket. He didn't even seem to notice that Sprog had put them there. Sprog was a bit disappointed, but perhaps the Boy just didn't understand about money.

Next morning, Sprog gave himself an extra good wash, using water they'd collected in a tin under a leak in the roof. He combed his hair with his fingers and wore his anorak — it was a shade smarter than the jumble sale mac, and it wasn't raining. He stuck to the odd wellingtons only because his plimsoles had worn right out; Sprog wished he'd picked some shoes up at the sale.

The newsagent was pleased to see Sprog — perhaps the boy called Terry had caught pneumonia! The satchel was tighter and heavier this time and there were two extra streets to do.

Sprog had delivered half the papers when he suddenly found his way blocked. Three kids on bikes were waiting on a corner — regulars from the shop. There was a ginger-haired girl, a dark, curly headed boy with a sarky grin and a fat kid wearing a size-too-small school cap and a pair of Billy Bunter spectacles.

The three bikes formed a triangle round Sprog, making a steel cage. None of the kids said anything, only stared. Sprog felt like an insect about to have its wings torn off.

He tried to push past. "What are you picking on me for? I done nothing to you. I'm only delivering papers, same as you lot."

Nobody answered. The trap tightened and Sprog ripped the satchel from his shoulder and flung it straight at the girl. She lost her balance, her bicycle swerved and toppled — and Sprog got through.

Sprog ran, keeping to alleyways where he could, steadily working uphill away from the town. The sloppy wellingtons began to chafe his legs, so he took them off and ran in his socks.

Sprog thought he'd shaken the kids off, too. He found the stretch of old railway and leapt along the sleepers. At the edge of the waste ground he pulled the wellingtons back on and then, keeping his head down, made for the warehouse. He had hardly closed the recess door when the bombardment began.

Stones rattled, bricks thumped on the double doors, a stick slithered and rattled down the sloping roof glass. Then there was a shoulder charge on the doors, making the big bar jump in its brackets.

The Boy sat awake beneath the cart, eyes frozen on the doors. The dog bristled and growled. Sprog said, "A load of kids out there, mate. They set on me down town, then they must have follered me up, somehow." Sprog wedged the recess door with a stout piece of wood under the handle, but nobody ventured through the weeds to find that way in.

The attack ceased as suddenly as it had started. A bicycle bell tinkled in the distance, followed by a derisive toot, but there were no voices.

The Boy's eyes glittered at Sprog. Sprog said, "Well, they've gone. So has me job. I can't go back to the shop no more. It's a shame really — I mean, it was a nice job. I reckon I'd have made fifteen pence today. Lousy kids! What did I do to them?"

Chapter Three

Had it been night time — even a night filled with hail and wind or some lurking terror — the Boy would have upped and gone, becoming a boy-shaped shadow lost in a world of shadows. Height or depth, cold and hunger, louse or rat — nothing diminished the Boy as the light did.

It was the day that sent him, cowed, into any dim refuge; shrank him, made his eyes big, bent his shoulders and froze his limbs. The Boy who was so brave and alive at night — this Boy faded as the sky lightened.

So now, in the face of an uncertain danger he would not run from, he lay quite still under his blanket with only the top half of his furrowed face showing, his eyes questioning upon Sprog. Sprog took a swig of fresh milk and nibbled at meaty bits of raw bacon, throwing the fat to the dog. He didn't look at the Boy but said, "They was only chucking stones. So what? You can chuck stones miles." He didn't dwell on the fact that some of the gang had tried to yank the big doors off their hinges.

"They're all at school now, doing their sums and saying their prayers. All the same, mate, better safe than sorry. When I nip off, bung the bit of wood back against the door. I'll give me secret signal when I come back."

Sprog's nonchalance evidently pacified the Boy, but the dog stayed uneasy, fixing its eyes upon Sprog in

silent reproach as he let himself out. The mutt sometimes lived bits of the Boy's life for him.

Sprog found a different way into town, keeping well
clear of the newsagent's shop. He thought of slipping in
and trying to explain what had happened, but there
wasn't much point: he wouldn't get his job back. Those
kids would have returned the satchel with its undeliver-
ed newspapers, then, most likely, told a lot of fairy tales
about Sprog.

A leaden sky brooded over the streets, but it didn't
rain all morning. Sprog kept on the move, on the look
out for pickings and happenings. He kept clear of main
roads until midday when he could pretend to be just
another kid from school. He found little quiet spots on
the river front, spent some time at a mid-week market,
nicked a large packet of jam tarts, a small one of fruit
gums, a box of matches he thought might be useful and
blued half his money on a football badge he fancied.

After dinner (not that Sprog had dinner) he thought
of trying to wangle himself, for free, into the pictures —
Sprog had managed it before — only he'd seen the film.
During the afternoon it got colder, an east wind whirling
up the river and blowing rubbish about in the streets.
Sprog ran to keep warm, until the wellingtons chafed
again. He thought about shoes and sleeping bags; a
couple of sleeping bags were what he and the Boy would
need for winter nights, but neither shoes nor sleeping
bags grew on lamp posts. Anyway, with sleeping bags
you had to watch out for lice: you couldn't shake them
out so easily as you could from a blanket.

A lingering twilight set in soon after three and specks
of icy rain stung Sprog's face like the points of pins. At
a quarter to four the kids started coming out of school

— and that was when they got him.

Sprog was never sure whether they were the kids from the newspaper shop or a different lot. All he knew was that the street he was in became a trap. The cyclists swished in tight, small formations at each end, their faces half hidden behind scarves and the thick collars of duffle coats.

There was only one possible way of escape: an alley marked by white posts, cut between high brick walls glittering along the tops with broken glass. Sprog dived through.

The kids dismounted and threaded their way through the posts, bringing their machines. Sprog had gained a fair start on them, but he hadn't a chance on foot against the wheeled bikes. They wooshed behind him, owls on the wing, keeping a certain distance as if they knew their prey couldn't escape.

The alley grew darker the farther in it went, and the kids switched on probing lamps. Blinded, Sprog did not see the steps ahead, nor the figures squatting there, until he'd stumbled headlong into them. Somebody reached for him, not grabbing but shoving. The hand pushed him back towards the dazzle of cycle lamps — they wanted him as pig-in-the-middle.

Sprog backed against the wall and shouted, "What are you lot on to me for? What have I done to you?"

The kids' reply came in the strident chords of bells and hooters — as if this strange, intimidating chorus was their only language.

Sprog plugged his ears with his fingers, then let fly with one foot. A kid who had come too close doubled up as the toe of a wellington sank into his belly. His cycle, lights aglow, stood against the wall at the foot of the steps and Sprog took off with it. He climbed the steps, up and up, dragging the machine clattering after him. At the top he found a narrow, deserted street behind the buildings. The bicycle was too big for him, but he bestraddled the cross bar, stood on the pedals and was away.

Away round the corner, then another and another. Then, by chance or instinct, he found the edge of the waste ground and reached the abandoned railway through a gap. He bumped the bike along the sleepers, sure of his direction. Above the open space the sky still held light and, against it, Sprog saw the tall, blunt shadow of the warehouse.

He braked, half fell off, then dragged the bike into the tall weeds beside the rails. Peering back he made out a cluster of lamps jigging about at the end of the street; then, one by one, they twinkled through the gap Sprog had found and came bobbing along the rails.

Sprog swore, dropped the bike in the weeds and plunged through towards the warehouse. Too late, he realized he'd forgotten to switch off the lamps on the borrowed bicycle. Two pools of light, yellow and red, shone in the dark grass — a dead give away!

Then new ideas flashed through Sprog's mind as he ran for the recess door. The kids probably didn't need a beacon to guide them — they'd known all along where he was heading, they'd rumbled the hideout. Picking Sprog up in town had been just part of some game — only they'd had all the fun. Did the kids know about the Boy, too — even the mutt? The raided milkcarts, the clothes nicked from washing lines, the night prowls . . . maybe word had got round. They were *all* blown! It was time for a new journey into nowhere.

Sprog tapped out his signal and the Boy took his time about coming and removing the wedge. He let Sprog in, but retreated at once to his funk hole beneath the cart.

Sprog didn't waste time resecuring the door. He began stuffing his bits and pieces into the duffle bag.

"The whole town's on its way up, mate," he said. "Get packed — we're moving, fast."

The Boy's eyes glittered back at Sprog then made their familiar switch up to the roof glass. Away from the alleys, far above the tangled grass, the wintry sky was loath to sleep.

"Soon be pitch dark," said Sprog. "Stars are out already," he lied. "What're we waiting for?"

The Boy hunched his knees, hugging them, knuckles tight. He couldn't seem to unlock his eyes from the roof. Sprog couldn't read much in the face so he looked at the dog instead; eyes like brown pebbles turned on the Boy, waiting; ears cocked for sound, tail twitching — waiting . . .

Sprog pulled the duffle strings tight and swung the bag on his shoulder. "I'm off, mate," he said. "I'm not stopping here to be torn to pieces by that lot. Look, I'll wait for you across the waste ground. I'll wait, see?" Then Sprog went out.

In the direction of the railway tracks the lights were bobbing nearer and nearer. The vanguard, by now, was directly opposite the warehouse, across the tall grass. Sprog knew he'd been spotted. The bells and hooters started up again and cycle lamps clove through the half-darkness trying to pick him out as he ran — ran and ran through the undergrowth in a wide arc away from the warehouse.

Two of the gang broke away and came after him.

Sprog ran twisting down the narrow path to the street, panting with cold night air in his lungs, not slowing until he was sure he'd shaken off pursuit.

Sprog had not waited for the Boy. At length he found himself in a broad, house-lined avenue bright with street lamps — a quiet road away from the town, away from the river. He limped along the pavement, a small anonymous speck of guilt and self hate. The Boy felt so close that he was like a parrot sitting on Sprog's shoulder.

Sprog said out loud, "Didn't you understand what I was saying, mate? I *wanted* you to come, honest! I never meant to run out on you, but you wouldn't shift, see?"

The claws tightened on his shoulder.

The avenue ran out of lights, the smooth pavement vanished and became a scarred rut of rough stones and mud deeply etched with heavy tyre patterns. In front of a half built house a giant cement mixer kept a lonely vigil.

Sprog cheered up quite a bit; he'd taken over building sites more than once in the past. Here there was a row of five detached houses in various stages of construction. The one at Sprog's extreme left was merely a shell of exposed bricks and gaping holes. The house at the other end was roofed and glazed and had net curtains sagging across front windows, though no light shone.

Sprog picked the middle house of the five. The roof seemed all there and they'd started on the windows. A shove at the locked door got Sprog nowhere, but when he crept cautiously through builders' debris round to the back he had better luck. The back door hung on hinges but there were no other fittings. A small wedge had been used to keep it shut. Sprog opened it and went upstairs to bed. Off the upper landing new doors stood open, one into an unfinished toilet, others into larger rooms. Sprog tried them all, kicking into obstructions, sniffing at new wood and paint, striking matches as he went.

There was no glass in the windows up here and Sprog waited till he'd found a room in which his latest match did not at once gutter out. He peered out of the window space down into the untidy darkness of somebody's future back garden and reckoned that, if it came to the pinch, he could jump it. It might be a bit warmer downstairs, but if anyone came on the prowl Sprog would have less chance of bolting for it through either the front or back doors. This was a better look-out post, too.

In the lee of the wind, Sprog undid his duffle bag and got out his blanket. He rolled himself in this, then dug in the bag, coming up with half a bar of chocolate and a bruised apple.

Sprog fell asleep before he finished the apple. He dreamed vividly of the Boy: they were all trapped in the warehouse — Sprog, Boy and mutt — with the walls and roof falling in and kids on bicycles pouring through the gaps in endless waves, pedals whirling, wheels spinning, bells and hooters full blast. None of the kids had faces, but the Boy had a new face — a face Sprog had never seen before. A wide nose, slanted eyes — and a mouth which formed a scream, but you couldn't hear it because the kids were kicking up all that row.

The mutt was barking, not with its familiar, nervous yap but upon the deep, snarling note of a hound straining at a leash . . .

Sprog was suddenly sharply awake, staring up at the open window space. He was vaguely but unpleasantly aware of some menace which lurked out there in the night, something he had partially met in his dream.

Then a dog barked, followed by a man saying something short and unintelligible. A chain rattled. The dog yelped.

Sprog disentangled himself from his blanket and crept to the window. A bright half moon shone frostily on the rough ground below and Sprog glimpsed movement behind the bone-white willow fence enclosing the future garden.

Sprog ducked, far too late, behind the sill. A torch beam as powerful as a searchlight had swept across the window and caught Sprog full in the face.

The dog barked and the man barked back. The chain gave a final rattle and there was the scud of huge paws across rough ground — Sprog half expected a grizzly bear to come leaping clean through the window!

Sprog wriggled away, crawling on hands and knees, groped for the way out and retreated backwards across the splintery landing into a room at the front — perhaps he could jump from there.

A bundle of pipes, leaning against the wall, toppled with ear shattering impact. The dog came bounding up the stairs. Sprog kicked the door closed, got his fingers under the string securing the pipes and heaved them against the door. The door bent inwards but held out against the massive paws scratching frantically at the panels. Heavy footsteps sounded on the landing and a shoulder added its weight to the straining door. There was a grunt of command, the rattle of the chain, the clip of a fastening — then Sprog and pipes were uprooted as the door flew in.

"On your feet!"

Impaled in the torch beam, Sprog obeyed. The dog — or its shadow — sat temporarily cowed at the man's feet. Patience was not its strong point, though. Now and then it gave a vicious lunge forward, tightening the chain, fangs gleaming — until the man flicked at it with the stout leather thong of the lead handle.

Sprog's human captor wore the peaked hat and grey uniform of a security guard and his shoulders looked six feet wide. "What are you doing in here, sonny?" he demanded.

"Just having a kip," said Sprog.

The torch beam swept from corner to corner. "What else have you been up to? Busted any windows? Wee-ed on the paint work? Let's have the truth."

"Nothing," said Sprog. "I done nothing, only had a kip."

"Well, you can finish that down at the police station. You keep walking ahead of me down the stairs. And don't try anything clever. This is a nasty brute I've got here — a killer, if you give him the chance. He eats little boys like you every morning for breakfast."

Sprog sat in the passenger seat of a waiting van, with the door locked and the watchdog breathing throatily through a grille behind him. The security guard used his radio. "They're sending somebody to collect you, sonny," he said. "Just sit there and be a good boy, eh?"

"I've left me gear behind — in the house," said Sprog.

The guard relaxed. He sat big and kind and jokey beside Sprog.

"What, your feather bed and colour TV? They'll

keep. Where're you from?"

"Just around," said Sprog.

Eyes settled on Sprog in the pale moonlight.

"You ought to be tucked up safe at home, a kid like you."

"I was," said Sprog. "Till you come along."

"One of the cheeky ones, eh?" chuckled the guard, not taking offence. "You on the run from somewhere?"

"Who, me?"

"What's your name?"

"Sprog," said Sprog.

"Not very old, are you?"

Sprog didn't have to answer. Headlights swept the road. A police patrol car pulled up beside the van, blue light flashing.

The driver got out and crossed to the van's windows. "What have you got this time, chum?" he asked the guard.

"About three feet nothing and full of back chat. He isn't armed, and no damage done. He's all yours."

"Hello, lad," said the policeman. "Got yourself in a spot of bother have you?" He sounded young and cheerful and matter of fact. "Fancy a ride in a police car?"

"Can I go back and fetch me gear?" asked Sprog.

"Gear?"

"Me bedding and that."

The policeman thought that was funny for some reason, but he took Sprog back into the house, holding his hand. It felt funny, somebody holding Sprog's hand.

"No handcuffs?" asked Sprog.

The young policeman said, patiently, "You won't try kicking my shins or biting my wrist, will you? I'd have to be nasty, if you did that. You wouldn't want me to be nasty."

Upstairs, Sprog took his time about rolling up his blanket and stuffing it into the duffle bag. "Give us a bit of light, eh?"

The policeman obligingly shone his torch. Sprog saw that he had left nothing behind — except the half eaten apple. He heaved the duffle bag on his shoulder and nodded. "That's the lot, ta — reckon they'll give me supper down at the nick?"

"Breakfast more likely," said the policeman. "If you're nice and polite to the station sergeant."

Chapter Four

"Bag?" said the station sergeant. He watched without much enthusiasm as Sprog tipped out blanket, comics, chocolate wrappings and this and that. "Now your pockets?"

He found Sprog's half full box of matches more interesting. "You a smoker?"

"Not really," said Sprog.

The sergeant took another close look at Sprog's face before asking, "Run around on your own, do you?"

"Yeah."

"*Always* on your own?"

"Well . . . yeah, more or less."

"Not with another kid — and a dog?"

Sprog came up with the answer pat: "Don't like dogs, much."

The policeman studied Sprog's innocence, gave the match box a rattle, then placed it carefully on the folded blanket. He was an older, stouter policeman, face red from the heat of a gas fire behind the counter. Instead of troubling to turn the fire down, he'd taken off his tunic and hung it on the back of a chair. Wide braces heaved a pair of huge trousers snug against an ample stomach.

He returned to his desk and took a swig out of a cracked mug and the next bite of a sugary doughnut. He saw Sprog enviously looking on and said, "Hungry?" He got up and crossed to a door. "Hey, Bill," he called. "Rustle up this kid some breakfast, will you?"

It was getting light, now — gone seven by the clock on the wall. The sergeant came back and looked sternly down upon Sprog.

"We have to find out who you are, see?"

The question didn't make much sense to Sprog.

"I know who I am."

"Sprog," said the policeman, as if it was a mild joke. "That's not a name."

"It's okay," said Sprog.

"Not for me, it isn't. You belong somewhere, or to somebody. That's what we've got to find out, only you won't tell. Everybody belongs somewhere."

A constable came in with a tray. There was a plate of cornflakes heaped with sugar and two pieces of crisp toast and a saucer with marmalade in it.

The sergeant watched, not unkindly but not wanting any nonsense, either. "Well, get yourself outside that lot. I'll do most of the talking till you've done."

"Ta," said Sprog. He didn't feel sulky or resentful. It had been a fair cop and they hadn't caught him nicking anything. For the moment he didn't even want to escape — not till after breakfast, anyway.

The sergeant sat at the other end of the table, apparently sharing Sprog's pleasure. When Sprog was still half way through his cornflakes he drew a writing pad towards him. His ball pen clicked.

"Now let's have another try," he said. "You don't have to talk much with your mouth full. Just nod or shake your head. I'll do a bit of thinking aloud, right?"

Sprog nodded. The sergeant went on. "You're a Londoner. I'm no detective, but I can guess that much. I can guess by the way you talk — *when* you talk — and the way you move about. And I wouldn't say you were a bad boy — I can tell that, too. We get quite a lot of bad boys in here, you know. On the other hand, you must have been in a bit of trouble, somewhere. Somewhere in London? Why not let me into the Secret? You don't think we'd whip you off to Borstal, just because you nicked a few peanuts? It's all for your own good — you must see that. You're not stupid. We can't have kids like you adrift, floating about, wandering off nowhere in particular. Unhappy at home, were you?" Sprog shook his head, spreading marmalade thickly on his toast.

"Father belt you? Come on, let's have it. And hurry it up. I'm off duty soon, and the copper who takes over from me has a different way with kids."

It was then that Sprog grew aware of a different set of sounds. Barking dogs! Barking, yelping, howling dogs somewhere behind the police station. And, more important, there was one very special, familiar yap that Sprog's sharp ears would have picked out had it wafted all the way from Australia.

Sprog felt a tingle down his backbone. Only one dog emitted that pathetic, heart-rending cross between a woof and a whine when it wanted to be let out. The mutt!

Sprog went on taking his time over breakfast. The sergeant's pad stayed blank, except for the little drawings he was making in one corner — lots of question marks joined together into an elaborate pattern.

The morning got brighter and busier and there was a lot of coming and going. Eventually the station sergeant clicked at his ball pen, gave Sprog a sad, disillusioned,

I-wash-my-hands-of-you expression, then greeted a new-comer — a slim, ramrod-backed person wearing a pip on each shoulder and a moustache like a shoe brush. They both looked at Sprog and Sprog looked — a trifle too longingly — at the street door.

"Forget it," said the police inspector. "You're not going anywhere — until I send you."

He was too busy to bother with Sprog after that. A small battery of telephones opened fire and, to judge from the activity, there had just been a million pound bank robbery round the corner.

And then, threading his way through the confusion, carefully avoiding flying uniforms, a kid came in from the street. Sprog recognized him at once as one of the roundsboys from the newsagent's — the kid with the school cap and Billy Bunter specs. He had a satchel full of papers which he laid on the counter.

The roundsboy saw Sprog, clearly under arrest, and smirked. Then he took a couple of papers out of the satchel, left his cap beside it and trundled up some stairs. Presumably he was delivering the papers to one of the offices — perhaps even to the Superintendent of Police, which would account for the polite removal of the cap.

Sprog saw that nobody had their eyes on him at that moment. He grabbed the satchel of papers, rammed the school cap on his head and took half a dozen rapid strides into the corridor at the back of the office. He'd kept his duffle bag, though the blanket and other things had been taken away. He hid the bag in the satchel.

He ignored the stairs and kept on going to a fire door at the end of the corridor. He carefully pushed the bar and let himself through and just as carefully closed the door behind him.

Sprog was in a smallish square yard with the sound of barking now very close and clamorous. The kennels were to his right and the mutt's cell was the third cubicle along behind a thick, wire-mesh gate with a latch. The mongrel, which rarely showed affection for anyone other than the Boy, simply sniffed in recognition and limped through the gate and out across the yard, then vanished.

Sprog found the yard gate leading into a walled driveway. A police car sat just inside off the main road, window wound down, radio tweeting, driver watching Sprog's approach. Sprog walked towards it, whistling. "Paper?" he enquired.

The policeman felt for a coin. *"Express"*

Sprog handed over the newspaper, pocketed the coin, resumed whistling and turned into the main street. Hurrying feet and a bridge spanning the road indicated to Sprog the nearness of a railway station. He went up the approach, carried with the crowd, and chose a pitch well away from book stalls and close to the station entrance.

"Papers," he called, huskily. "Read all about it!" He'd sold the lot in three minutes flat.

An unbelievable fortune in coins jingling in his pocket, Sprog set off against the tide of morning travellers. Almost too late, he spotted a couple of paper round kids waiting at the foot of the approach — the fat one missing his cap, of course!

Sprog tried melting into the solid wall but lost himself amongst legs and folded umbrellas instead. At the bottom of the railway approach he rescued his empty duffle bag, hung the satchel on a railing and stuck the school cap on the spike beside it.

He'd put half a dozen streets and alleys between himself and the scene of his crime when he saw the dog hobbling ahead. To have lost Sprog in that brick landscape, then made a miraculous reappearance once the hue and cry had died down, was the sort of agile deceit the mutt was capable of.

Sprog followed the dog. Now that he was on the loose again, Sprog's mind returned to the fate of the Boy. He got close enough to ask the dog, "What happened to him? Did he get clear? How come you got nicked by the coppers?" But the mutt wasn't talking.

It was possible, if not all that likely, that the dog had run out on the Boy, too. Now it was attaching itself to Sprog, on the spree, shaking off the smell of gaol and Sprog could tag along if he liked — or if he could. Yet the mongrel's three-legged progress had about it a galvanized sense of mission — limping on, briefly stopping, glancing back, hobbling on again, stopping . . . Wherever it was going it was not uphill to the warehouse.

Dark clouds curled overhead, thicker than smoke, hastening in the same direction as the dog. The dog got to the end of the street, turned a corner and wriggled under a wooden fence, leaving its tail in evidence just long enough for Sprog to spot it. Sprog did not crawl after the dog, but went along the fence until it became a set of railings and then an iron gate. By then, the mutt had cut across from the fence and was scrambling awkwardly down a flight of rough, stone steps — to the river.

The littered quay held only the echoes of river sound;

it was as deserted and idle as the old railway high above — very much the mutt's kind of place. It was sniffing, now, at the foot of a huge derelict crane with rusty bogies set in rusty tracks. It gave Sprog its familiar backward, pathetic stare and, when Sprog did not move, uttered a series of shrill, whimpering barks.

"Pack it in," said Sprog. "You'll get us both nicked again if you keep that up."

Sprog thought of finding a piece of rope, tying the dog to it and dragging it off with him. It seemed a shame to let it run loose. He tried whistling for it but the mongrel stayed obstinately rooted, its front paws planted on one of the wheels. The droop of tail expressed a baffled sense of grievance and when Sprog walked out on it the dog made no move to follow.

Sprog climbed the steps and decided to take a look at the warehouse. It was risky but the kids were all in school, now, and the waste ground was as unpopulated as the moon. If only he could get some idea of what had happened to the Boy and why his mutt was hanging about, lost, by the river . . .

It took a while for Sprog to get his bearings and rediscover their old hideout. The shell of building looked much the same from a distance, but when he'd made a cautious approach through the undergrowth he saw that the recess door had been broken in and, from the jagged opening, came the lingering stench of smoke.

There had been a fire, all right. Charred wood, burnt sacks in the recess where their beds had been; one side of the old cart scorched . . . and the cobbled floor was still running with too much water for rain. It had gushed from a fireman's hose, more likely.

The Boy had tried to stay put, so they had smoked

him out. The Boy who was frightened of the light was even more terrified of fire. The kids couldn't have known that, yet they'd hit on the one trick that would flush him, terrified, into the open.

For a moment Sprog thought the Boy·was still there, squatting asleep with his back to the shadowed partition, against a sodden heap of blackened sacks. But it was only the knitted hat Sprog had once given him, hung on a nail. Sprog took it down and stuffed it into his duffle bag.

"*Always* on your own?" the station sergeant had asked, thoughtfully shaking Sprog's matches. "Not with another kid — and a dog?"

The coppers had got the dog, but if they'd captured the Boy too wouldn't the sergeant have made some remark about the disfigured face — pity, perhaps, or extra curiosity — in his expression?

Not that it made much difference, now, to Sprog. "Yeah," Sprog could have answered, truthfully. "On me own. There's no other kid."

Chapter Five

So Sprog was a loner again. He had money in his pockets from the papers he had sold, but his nearly empty duffle bag hung limp upon his shoulder and it would need replenishing.

With new rain threatening in the sky, Sprog got clear of the wasteground and hopped on the first bus that came by. He would have paid his fare, only the conductor saw him neither come nor go.

Sprog sat in an upstairs seat for ten minutes. The bus followed a route never far from crane jibs and fleeting glimpses of shiny water between buildings. When a new line of shops began, Sprog hopped off.

He spent a cold, dangerous, but not entirely unprofitable day in the streets. The shop windows were merry with Christmas decorations and bright Christmas trees. He stole biscuits, bananas, a couple of pork pies and a large bag of sweets, stuffing them all into his duffle bag as he went.

He blued some of his money on a new torch with a spotlight beam. He wondered whether to buy some shoes, but they cost too much and the odd wellingtons were comfortable enough wedged with paper. Besides, it started raining again. The jumble sale mac leaked. His hair got soaked and icy water trickled up his cuffs and down his neck. He could have done with a scarf.

In the afternoon he used up nearly all the rest of his

money on the pictures. Virtuously clutching his ticket, he groped his way to a seat in the middle of the empty stalls. There he steamed contentedly, munched through one of the meat pies and rustled open the bag of sweets.

The film was a Western and Sprog was transported to Arizona, basking in an alien, golden sun. Bullets whined at someone else across the silvery screen, so that for the time being Sprog utterly forgot that he was an outlaw, he, too, a marked man.

Sprog saw the film round again and when he came out, it was night once more. It had stopped raining and the coloured lights, festooned along the shop fronts, gave the real wintry world of the town a touch of tinsel fantasy — until Sprog, not sure where to go next, left the lights behind.

Sprog had his own kind of wilderness and, although he had never been at the wrong end of a Winchester 73, running was often his only illusion of freedom, distance the only hiding place.

Heaving his heavier duffle bag on his shoulder, Sprog hopped on another bus, a bus taking him back to the point where he had started. At first, he did not know why he was going back. It was not the thrill of danger, much less any hope of a bed for the night. He gazed out of the upper-deck window, watching the blood red navigation lights of cranes dart across the sky, brighter and faster than shooting stars. It was funny about the mutt, he was thinking, wondering why he hadn't thought it before. Had it gone crazy? Did dogs go crazy — like people?

Sprog got off the bus, having paid the fare with the last of his money, and soon his wellingtons fell softly on a remembered pavement lit by fuzzy lamps.

At the iron gate leading down to the quay Sprog tried

out his new torch, sending the sharp beam scorching down the steep steps. Hearing no close sound he followed the beam down and wondered why he was bothering. There was nobody there, *nothing* there — except the old crane and a tug pulling a short train of barges along the light-flecked river.

Then the dog came out of the shadows, out of some hiding place, its eyes sharp and welcoming in Sprog's torchlight. It rubbed itself against Sprog's wellingtons then ran to the foot of the crane and looked back.

A pale elongated patch of light moved at Sprog's feet. At first he couldn't see where the light had come from. Then, in the corner of his eye, he saw a speck of bright starlight above his head. He stared up — up the endless girders of the old crane. They receded into darkness, but the star winked at the top, on and off, on and off . . .

Then Sprog knew! Going part way round the foot of the crane he found the beginning of an iron ladder. He began climbing up the ladder. The wind from the river caught him and buffeted him in vicious, sideways blows and his arms and hands were pierced by unseen icicles.

Sprog took one quick glance down, but saw nothing. His feet tapered away into shadows and the dog wasn't following — not up that Jacob's ladder. Through the sigh of the wind he heard its urgent, defeated yelping. Above Sprog the star grew bigger, shed a beam on his face, became a bright lens. Then at last he ran out of rungs.

The Boy was kneeling on a perilously narrow platform at the top of the ladder. He offered Sprog a thin hand, ice in ice, and drew him beside him. Sprog knelt a moment on the platform, regaining his breath.

The Boy's face was bathed in a deep, red glow from a

navigation light. The wind sighed in their ears and cut through their clothing and Sprog knew that if he spoke his words would be lost. He waited until the Boy pushed open a door, then he followed him in.

The door shut the wind out and Sprog said, "Where did you dream this place up from, mate?"

The Boy switched on his torch again and flashed it once at Sprog and then more slowly round the interior of the cabin, as though showing it off. One wall was a mass of dials and levers with, in front, a couple of swivel seats. A strip of coconut matting lay on the floor with the Boy's tartan blanket stretched across it. There must have been observation windows all round the cabin at one time — long since smashed and roughly boarded up. The only view was through chinks and one tiny window above the dials giving a faint view of the jib. There was dust and cobwebs and the smell of oil.

"I reckoned you'd got away all right," said Sprog. "How did you know I was down there? Was you expecting me back?" What he meant was, did you *want* me back?

Sprog swung himself into one of the chairs and began unloading his duffle bag. The Boy evidently hadn't yet got round to stocking a larder. Sprog broke the last meat pie in half, flung the Boy the hat he had rescued and began telling his story: "I bust out of the nick this morning. I sprung your mutt and all. Did you know the coppers had him? And what do you think? I flogged some newspapers at the staion. Spent all me money, though."

The Boy responded, as ever, only in his breathing and with those flashes of quick eyes. Sprog went on, "What we going to do about your dog? He's doing his nut down there at the bottom. If he goes on kicking up a row like that, he'll bring out the cavalry."

The Boy ate his pie, apparently unperturbed. Sprog went on relating his adventures but the Boy had got tired of listening. He was swinging slowly to and fro in the other chair, peering through a crack in the window boards. At first, Sprog thought he was searching for his dog down on the quay, but when he found a peephole of his own next to the Boy's, all he could see was the flowing river. The Boy seemed obsessed with the reflected lights on the sluggish water far beneath them.

Sprog said, as a sort of joke, "What d'you want to do, mate? Jump in? Well, I suppose we could do worse. It's going to get perishing cold up here, i'n it?"

They went to bed on the mat, eventually. Having lost his blanket, Sprog had to hunt round for some alternative covering. He came up with a few bits and pieces left behind by workmen — a man's jacket, a pair of greasy overalls and a piece of stiff canvas.

During the night the wind got up, shrieking through the window boards, and the cabin began to sway so much that Sprog, startled awake, felt sure the crane was toppling over.

When the Boy shook him Sprog knew that it was just before dawn.

"We off already?" he asked, sleepily. "I thought we might stop here for Christmas."

The wind had eased off. They got their things together and prepared for the long descent down Jacob's ladder.

The Boy pushed open the cabin door and two seagulls were disturbed on the little platform outside. They swept off in a frenzy of surprise. "Have they laid any eggs?" asked Sprog. "I wouldn't mind an egg for me breakfast."

The air clung to them like coats of frost as they made their way down, the Boy going first, and the steel in their palms felt sharp enough to cut to the bone.

A disused garage, the back of a wrecked van, an air-raid shelter buried like a mass grave at the edge of a park — these were among their sleeping places before the true winter fell from heavy skies.

Holing up was never easy together, with the Boy preferring to roam at night and Sprog by day. They never got started on a real journey but, avoiding the immediate district where they had hit trouble, drifted ever deeper into derelict regions along the riverside — covering no more than a couple of miles in a week.

They spent Christmas in a railway cattle truck, one of a short train parked in a marshalling yard. There were straw bales at one end, the floor was scattered with loose straw and the not unpleasant country smell was an improvement on drains, diesel oil and rats' droppings. They curled themselves up like hamsters to sleep and Sprog reckoned it was the best bed he `had ever "kipped" in.

Sprog shopped around on Christmas Eve and came back, zig-zag across the rails, with his duffle bag full of fruit, pies, packets of sweets and several cans of shandy and beer.

On Christmas morning — the Boy and his dog had stayed put for once — Sprog kept remembering things. Perhaps it was eating mince pies for breakfast that started it. Sprog said, "We used to have Christmas at the Home. We had a real dinner, with turkey and baked spuds and crackers, and we all put on funny hats. We had Christmas pud for afters, of course — I never come across no Christmas pud yesterday, on the nick. Still, we got the mince pies — wouldn't mind a bit of custard to go with mine. Want another pie?"

The Boy had given most of his first one to the dog but it had only sniffed at it and slyly buried it in the straw. The mutt rarely ate anything unless it was out of a dustbin.

The Boy didn't want the last pie so Sprog ate it.

"We went out carol singing, sometimes," he went on. "A big bunch of us, standing under a street lamp. Matron's hubby used to play the accordion. Wasn't bad on it, neither. Some of us took turns to knock on doors and collect the money." Sprog emptied his mouth thoughtfully. "You and me could have done that — gone carol singing, I mean. You can get a lot of shekels, carol singing . . . "

The Boy just sat there, cross-legged on his heap of straw, either listening or thinking. Anyway, it had been a stupid idea — Sprog couldn't see the Boy singing carols. Come to that, he couldn't see himself singing in the street, either. And he'd forgotten all the words, too, except for a fragment the kids had sung, taking the rise out of Matron: "While shepherds washed their socks by night . . . "

"We might have tagged on with some other kids, carol singing," Sprog persisted. "They wouldn't have noticed us in the dark."

Christmas Day lasted a long time. The Boy went to sleep, the mutt snoozed, Sprog dozed. Some time in the afternoon he woke up and started on the beer. He soon got a swimmy head but instead of it being funny it brought twirly images into Sprog's mind. People across the tracks, people in lighted houses screaming with laughter, people having the time of their lives. Everybody at home, everybody eating Christmas dinner, everybody wearing funny hats. Sprog fancied a party, but how could you have a party with *them*?

He gave the stirring Boy a sour, disgusted look, and he suddenly wanted to cry in anger and misery. Ugly mush! Why didn't he hop it and take his mutt with him? He could leave some of his clothes behind, if he liked. Sprog could always stuff them with straw and sit them against the wall of the cattle truck — what would be the difference?

"Wouldn't mind a game of cards," said Sprog, swigging the beer. "I'd teach you rummy, only we haven't got any cards."

The Boy was lying back, head cradled in hands, eyes blank and unblinking. Then, at some distant sound to which Sprog attached no importance, they both sat up, Boy and dog, eyes haunted.

"What're you listening for — Santa Claus?" jeered Sprog, and he began to sing aloud, not very tunefully, "Jingle bells, Jingle bells . . . "

When Sprog awoke, his head was still spinning. The truck was pitch dark save for a sliver of moonlight cutting through a crack in the doors. He knew at once that the Boy and his dog had gone.

Sprog switched his torch on, slid open the door and dropped down beside the track, desperately needing the toilet. The big moon was like a ball of frost in an icy sky.

Sprog was violently sick into a patch of frozen weeds. He crawled back to the cattle truck, shivering, and nestled into his straw heap.

He had noticed no activity near the tracks and yet, before Sprog was quite asleep again, the truck began to move. There was a series of jerks, buffer clanging on buffer, and the wheels under Sprog gathered speed, grinding on their rails.

The door rasped open and a lithe, swift figure flew in, its only sound a familiar high-pitched whistle. The dog leapt in after the Boy. Sprog, properly awake now, sat up and saw the shadow of the Boy sitting in its usual place, apprehensive but not inclined to action.

"You nearly missed the train, mate!" said Sprog. "What do we do now? Jump for it?"

But a ride was a ride to somewhere, so they sat it out. A long, smooth ride — until there was a final jerk, a sharp exclamation of steel on steel, and the truck seemed to glide off on its own until it crawled to a squeaking stand-still.

They waited a minute. At last, the Boy pushed at the door and peered out, to and fro; a quick eye-flash at Sprog and he was off, the dog melting with him into the moonlight.

Sprog grabbed his duffle bag and climbed down. There was nobody near, no voice came after them. Across the tracks was a stretch of flat land silver with frost, crisp and crackling under Sprog's wellingtons.

Chapter Six

They were making a journey into silence. The frosty moon lit no roof, marked out no street. The river was behind them, a life-line to a space ship — but here was space and Sprog, gasping every time he opened his mouth, was unusually mute. His thoughts were unaccustomedly bleak, too. Suppose they got stuck in the open — all night? Trudging, trudging to nowhere . . . Sprog, thin mac over torn anorak, sensed a peril he had not met before: exposure to the utter cold. He wondered if even the Boy sensed it.

It was never easy to guess how the Boy felt, but his style of progress was a pointer. The Boy excited, or shaking off pursuit, would stay far ahead of Sprog for ever quickening his pace and compelling Sprog to run in order to keep him in sight. The Boy, companionable, would drop in beside Sprog, walking close, sharing mutely the brief moments of innocence.

But now, the second the white moon slid behind cloud, he began dragging behind Sprog and this showed that he was, for once, at a loss.

Sprog tried to watch the mutt. The dog was a sure clue to how the Boy was feeling — and the dog was unhappy. It kept darting short distances across the frozen waste, and then it would come hobbling back as though startled by apparitions, ears angled back, tail dangled stiff like a short length of frozen rope. It was limping badly — it always limped worse when it was low spirited. It was hungry, too: it would come across some scrap of edible rubbish in the coarse, frozen grass and try to turn it over with its paw where it lay tightly bonded to the ground.

A stiff, icy breeze blew into their backs from the river. Sprog said, through half closed lips, "A right touch of Siberia, isn't it mate? Got any ideas?"

For once it was Sprog's idea — or perhaps the mongrel's: a fence loomed high and close. The dog stood up against it on its one good hind leg, pawing at the planks and whining very softly. Rising on his toes, Sprog could just grasp the top of the fence. He heaved himself up, cocked a leg over, slithered down and made a soft landing on a spongy heap smelling of rotten vegetables.

Sprog crouched, waiting for the Boy. He came but without the dog — that would have to make its own way through, if there was one.

They were in a garden, long and narrow and marked at the end by lights glowing through curtains. The Boy's eyes shone at Sprog in enquiry and Sprog, keeping low, made for an outbuilding which had oddly shining sides and a long, icy-wet roof of glass. A greenhouse!

Sprog had his torch ready. Fumbling with a door catch he threw a thin beam into the interior. The light picked out flowerpots and seed boxes on shelves. Spreading foliage brushed their faces as they crept in. The air struck warm and as headily fragrant as a tropical forest.

"Not bad, is it?" murmured Sprog, not without pride. "We can have a nice kip here."

They carefully shifted several large pots to clear extra

floor space — the slatted wood platforms and some empty sacks made good enough beds. The dog arrived, snuffling softly at the door, and the Boy let it in.

"Must be something to eat in here," whispered Sprog. "Tomatoes and that." His fumbling hands discovered nothing, however, except a plant bearing a mass of berries as hard as marbles. "Up at the Home," he went on, tone slightly disgruntled, "Matron's hubby used to grow grapes in a greenhouse same as this."

The Boy was sitting very still, eyes on the surrounding glass. Sprog couldn't see what was worrying him. It was dark enough, wasn't it? And nobody was likely to come from the house to pick berries in the middle of the night — Christmas night, too. Sprog switched off his torch and his thoughts of food, and lay content. From floor level he could see the twin, blue glows of oil heaters, one at each end. It was so quiet that he could almost hear the plants growing.

Daylight — on Boxing Day — and late according to Sprog's automatic brain clock! He sat up, head fuzzy — that was the carbon dioxide given off by the plants — unable to see out because of the misty glass on all sides.

The Boy was still asleep. The dog was restlessly sniffing at the flower pot on the floor.

Sprog listened, heard nothing, got up and tried the door catch. The greenhouse door was meant to open outwards but it wouldn't budge. Sprog pushed a few times and eventually, with a creak of its frame, it opened just wide enough for Sprog to discover what was holding it in place.

Snow! Thick, frozen snow drifted against the door. A glance at the grey, glass roof told him that snow was piled thick on that, too.

The Boy was awake now, watching. Sprog said, "It's been snowing. All night by the look of it. We can't get out, mate. The door's stuck."

The Boy's eyes filled with horror. Then, not far away, came scraping sounds. Sprog wiped one of the misty windows with his sleeve and peered out towards the house. A man was there, muffled in cap, scarf and thick coat, shovelling snow away. He was hacking determinedly at the packed, frozen snow with the blade of his shovel. Sprog ducked down, quickly.

The sounds ceased and Sprog risked another peep out.

"Bloke's gone indoors now," he said, adding, ruminatively. "To his breakfast, I expect — eggs and bacon and toast and marmalade. If he chucks out any bits for the birds, I bet I'll beat them to it — if I can get out."

The Boy had a go at the door, eyes wild. He was more brutal with it than Sprog, shoving with his shoulder so that it warped away at the top with a splintering crack. He tried pushing at the bottom with his toe.

"Watch it," said Sprog. "Don't want to bust nothing and have that bloke coming out here checking on his pansies." He looked up at the snow-packed roof and — as a bit of an authority on greenhouses — spotted the hinged ventilation hatch. "We might be able to push that open, only we'll have to mind we don't shove our hands clean through the glass. Hold on!"

The strange eyes pierced Sprog, then flicked from side to side and up. Windows . . . windows . . . !

Sprog made a pyramid of big flower pots, climbed up, steadied himself and shoved his palms against the vent frame. He got a good grip and pushed. The packed snow stayed tight on the vent — the frame might have been screwed shut. "We're not getting out this way, mate," panted Sprog.

The Boy came at him, pushing him clean off the pile of flower pots. The pots tumbled over and the Boy built them up again, stood on the pyramid, placed his hands on the frame and thumped at it until the whole greenhouse shook. "Steady on, mate," said Sprog, uneasy at the Boy's explosive violence.

The Boy uttered one of his rare, high-pitched, muted cries — like an animal in a trap. His arms were taut on the frame, now, like twin bars of sprung steel. Suddenly the vent gave way. Splintered wood, dislodged snow and bits of metal blasted free and the Boy, with one heave of powerful arms, was through. He slithered a little way, sprawled across the slanting roof on his stomach and dangled one arm through the gap.

Sprog fetched the kit and thrust each bundle through the shattered roof hole. The Boy grabbed them and sent them skidding down the roof to land in the snowy garden — on the side of the greenhouse away from the house.

Still the Boy waited. He wanted his mutt, as well! The dog tried to sneak away only there was nowhere for it to go. Sprog seized it in his arms, climbed back, wobbling, on the pots and managed to coax it through the gap, hoping it wouldn't cut itself to pieces. It jumped of its own accord off the roof.

The arm which helped Sprog through the vent was like the jib of a small crane. Sprog lowered what was left of the frame in place, slid on his bottom down the snow-packed roof, landed in the garden and picked up his duffle bag.

The Boy was already half over the fence. The bank of snow made the climb easier — even the mutt managed it without Sprog having to plant a toe in its rump. On the other side of the fence they cut a twisting trail across the frozen marsh, stumbling from tree to tree, bush to bush, snow-drift to snow-drift, footprints and pawprints making a crazy pattern.

Plodding towards the next somewhere, a long way behind the Boy, Sprog made himself a promise. He was never going to tangle with the Boy, that was for sure! Arms like that could snap you clean in half, like a matchstick.

For over a week, into the new year, there was no break in the weather. They stuck together more than usual, crouched for hours in any shelter they could get, reluctant to come out from beneath the meanest roof lest something should happen to prevent their getting back.

A shed in the middle of a frozen allotment, a sewage pipe howling with wind, like a giant whistle — full of the smell of gas. They took to huddling together, all three of them, on Sprog's ground sheet and under the only blanket they still possessed. They spent shivering days and nights in half sleep, waking in numbed torpor to face either another iron-grey day or a bleak and starless night.

"We're losing our touch, mate," said Sprog more than once. "We can do better than this."

A couple of times they did better: a shop basement, for instance, filled with cosy packing cases and a builders' hut with the lingering warmth of dead cinders thawing their numb bodies.

But both times something went wrong. The mutt tipped over one of the packing cases and brought the shop keeper down to investigate; an alerted watch dog pawed the door of the builders' shed and they had to make off blindly across a desert of scaffolding.

There was suddenly a jinx on them, no longer the whirl of bicycle wheels like hawks' wings but the endless whisper of snowflakes borne upon the back of a moaning wind. Footprints in the snow were all too easy to follow, shop doors stayed shut against the cold and windows were tightly fastened. There was also Sprog's unusual lapse of discretion.

Just inside the entrance to a supermarket, too desperate for once to worry about the TV scanner, Sprog, one morning, tried to smuggle out a loaf of bread under his mac. It slipped clean through his stiff hands, bounced twice on the floor and hit a pyramid of tinned vegetables, sending the whole lot clattering. Instead of making a bolt for it, Sprog tried to retrieve the loaf.

There was a hue and cry. Sprog's escape route was blocked by shopping trolleys and a big, beefy manager bore down on him — he only got clear by vaulting over a trolley and chucking the loaf in the man's face.

After that, hanging about near shops in daylight — even that grim, cloud-grey daylight — would have been asking for trouble. Pickings got even more scarce, and Sprog saw danger in each shadow, and every passing car seemed to bleep with a police radio.

Driven out of a refuge, hating every moment, the Boy occasionally tagged along with Sprog, even when it was not dark; in quiet, deserted places, though, keeping most of his face hidden behind an old scarf. He had caught a cold and his damaged nose was almost completely blocked. He had to breathe through his mouth behind the scarf, wheezing fretfully along a couple of paces behind Sprog, the crippled dog hobbling close behind him.

On New Year's Day they got hardly anything to eat at all and they were homeless again. Late in the afternoon they trudged along a narrow street bending alongside a railway viaduct. Sprog said, "We ought to try our luck some place else, mate. Hop a bus, say, or a truck. Should be easy, with everything moving slow — or what about another freight train?" Sprog had a golden memory of the cattle truck where they had spent Christmas.

It was at the end of the railway street, with darkness falling, that the Boy — perhaps pondering over what Sprog had said, if he'd understood it — suddenly woke out of his apathy and plunged ahead.

"What now?" asked Sprog. "Remembered something?" A pale hope stirred. The Boy gasped a meaningless sound into his scarf. Sprog dragged his weak legs after him.

The Boy was focusing his red-rimmed, lashless eyes across a fence upon a point higher up. Timber stacks! Sprog was not impressed — he silently detested the Boy's fancy to hide in places underground or places far above it.

The gates were shut. Neither the Boy nor Sprog tried climbing the gate, which was seven feet high and glittering with half-thawed ice. They worked their way along the fence, found a couple of loose planks and crawled through, pushing their bags in front. The dog slunk after them.

They climbed up to the fourth rack of stored timber.

Up there they had a roof over their heads, of sorts. The wind gathered strength and set up a continuous murmur along the wooden tunnel. Slowly and fumblingly they collected bits and pieces together to make some kind of wall against the wind. The Boy scrambled along and, after a search, came back dragging a stiff bundle of plastic sheeting. They beat it out flat as best they could, then made a curtain of it, wedging the corners between planks.

The newspapers under their thin clothes crackled like old bones as they squatted on the blanket in the dark shelter they had made. For a long time, Sprog said nothing. The Boy breathed raspingly. The dog fell asleep, twitching with uneasy dreams.

Sprog felt wide awake and oddly light-headed. His dreams were wakeful ones, concentrating all his senses: smell, touch, sight . . . as sharp and tantalizing in detail as hallucinations. Warm places, bright lights, plates filled with things that sizzled and bubbled, the chatter of human voices, indistinct but golden memories . . .

"Nothing to eat, is there?" he asked the darkness. And then, "I reckon we ought to turn ourselves in, mate. I mean, what's the point? What are we trying to prove? Where's it going to get us, stopping out here in the cold? I never thought about it before but . . . it's stupid, isn't it? Bleeding stupid."

The Boy's eyes woke briefly on Sprog, then he was alone again.

Chapter Seven

Sprog soon gave up trying to sleep. It was still early and he reckoned they'd made a mistake, holing up so soon. They should have made sure of their fodder, first.

In a momentary surge of optimism, it all suddenly seemed easy again. A few bright shops would be open in the streets and it wasn't all that cold now, was it? Sprog was sweating.

The Boy and his dog were huddled asleep. Sprog wriggled carefully from under the blanket and sat up. Behind him, the plastic curtain rattled like a sail and the wind sighed and snapped, bearing tiny specks of hard snow. Already the sweat on his hands was beginning to freeze and Sprog rubbed them briskly together. The Boy's muffled head was resting on Sprog's duffle bag, so he left it behind.

He made his way down to the foot of the timber stack, then crawled through the gap in the fence. Although the sky was black, the waste of snow dazzled him. The street stretched ahead, faintly lamplit, the ordinary houses on each side making black, jagged shapes like the dwellings of a ruined city.

Sprog's weakened legs soon found the snow hard going and, despite his previous wakefulness, long tendrils of sleep tried to drag him down. His heavy wellingtons, stumbling forward as if having a wayward life of their own, never got him to a main road.

Sprog had turned a corner when his nose picked up a tantalizingly familiar scent. Fish and chips!

Along the thick, white pavement ahead went a small, lone traveller. Sprog's legs seemed to set off in pursuit even before his brain gave the instructions — their ache matched the ache at the pit of his stomach. The short figure, laden hand to chin with white packages, hooded in duffle coat, scuffed unaware through the deep snow and didn't turn until it reached the next lamp post. Then a sixth sense must have warned him that something predatory was at his heels.

They faced each other in the snow-flecked light; Sprog, and a boy with plump features and a look back which was wary rather than afraid — yet Sprog's gaze kept him pinned to the lamp post.

"Give us a chip, mate," said Sprog.

The kid didn't answer. His one ungloved hand went to a hole in the top parcel — he'd been helping himself out of it all the way along. Slowly he drew out a long, succulent sliver of fried potato and shoved it whole into his mouth — he suddenly had the look of a fat fledgling swallowing a fat worm.

"Mean little basket," said Sprog.

The kid tried to back away, sidling round the lamp post, making for the dark. Sprog stuck a foot out and sent him sprawling in the snow.

The kid could have made off — it was the fish and chips Sprog was after. He got his hands round one of the scattered warm parcels, but the fly-away fledgling changed into a crow, cawing at Sprog and sinking its talons into his throat. Choking, Sprog chopped viciously at the kid's fingers, broke their grip and lashed out with his foot. The wellington caught the kid in his groin and he yelled.

Still the kid clung on, getting a fresh grip on Sprog's clothing. Sprog tried to drag himself clear — he'd lost the parcel — but the kid came with him, slithering on his knees, face upturned. It was an older, more wizened face than Sprog had seen under the lamp post: Sprog cut at it with the sharp edge of his palm — again and again, fighting dirty, pulses pounding, feet and fists pounding. Even the fish and chips were forgotten: Sprog just wanted to put down this clinging crow — hunger was hatred!

The long moments of dark violence passed; Sprog, already lost in the corridors of a sick nightmare, found things happening to him which were only partly real: the man's voice out of nowhere, the powerful grasp of big hands, the sudden dazzle of strange lights. He was sitting on a hard chair in a room he'd never known, and the blurred image of a burly man with heavy breath and husky voice was hovering over him.

"What's your name?"

"Sprog."

"What's that supposed to mean? A ruddy little hoodlum, that's what you are. I'm going to hand you straight over to the law."

A stout, quiet faced woman floated into the room and began laying knives and forks and plates on the table. She glanced at Sprog — in pity, indignation, uncertainty.

"Vicious little basket, aren't you?" said the man. "Where do you live?"

Sprog didn't answer. He felt hot again and there seemed to be two identical kids sitting in the other chair. The woman was dabbing at their faces with a blob of cotton wool. There was blood on it. Sprog thought, I never bashed him in the face, did I?

They all went out and left him alone. Sprog could have upped and gone, but he wasn't going anywhere. This was it, he was thinking: nice cosy place — he could fall asleep, easy, till the police car arrived. Maybe they'd give him a few chips, first an' all — only his throat felt sore and hot and he wasn't sure he'd be able to swallow them down.

Sprog heard voices in his thudding ears:

"What are we going to do with him?"

"I don't know yet."

"He don't look — right. Do you think he's mental or sick?"

"Pull the other one! He wasn't so daft that he didn't know what was in them newspapers. And he was fit enough to lam into Tommy."

"We'll have to do something," said the woman. "For his own good. The police . . . "

"I'm not trudging out to the phone box in this weather. I'll give him a good hiding and turn him loose."

"We can't do that . . . "

They came back with the newspaper parcels. The woman shared out fish and chips on to plates waiting on a white table cloth.

The man glared at Sprog as his own gaze wandered to the table. "You can keep your thieving eyes off that lot," he said. "Think yourself lucky we're not turning you in. Go on, beat it, off home, and don't ever show your filthy face round here again."

He held open a door and Sprog went back into the waiting night. He stumbled about in the snow for half an hour before he remembered the timber stack. It was only by chance that he found it, only the last of his strength and consciousness that got him up to bed.

A long, long night. A thousand sleeps in one. Dreams . . . fancies. Moments of icy reality entangled in a web of long, contradictory hours. Why was it, for instance, that sometimes when Sprog woke in the middle of the night a snowy daytime peeped through the cracks in the timbers?

Sometimes Sprog was in a snug, warm bed with a rail at the bottom against which he could twitch his bare, warm toes. Sometimes he sat up, choking, ice in his lungs, having the memory of some unknown, unspoken words of his own. Once he half awoke and knew that he was pushing with his hand against the sleeper beside him — so hard, so unyielding . . . The Boy was dead! The Boy was a stiff corpse beside him and that was why he didn't move . . . but it was only a pile of planks with a shroud of sacking. Where, then, was the Boy?

A living thing wriggled and nestled beside Sprog. That wasn't the Boy, either; it was the dog. The mutt had crept there, or been thrust there, and Sprog felt the warmth of its body and drifted back to sleep.

Once, deep in that long, strange night, Sprog was sure that the single blanket was wrapped round and round him so tight that he could scarcely move his arms or legs. *Where was the Boy?*

Later, Sprog knew that he had been talking in his sleep again and he found himself lifted up, cradled in strong arms, not once but again and again.

Again and again he saw the Boy's face above him, in darkness and then, mysteriously, in light — that scarred and dreadful face bringing to Sprog's fevered mind a contented consciousness transmuted at once into floating insensibility.

At last came a clearer awakening, Sprog opening his eyes with an instinct of impending morning. A new dawn chorus sang along the timber tunnel, but it was the chorus of the wind. Sprog had a glimpse of huge snow flakes falling like a speckled curtain across the far end of the tunnel.

He was sitting up between the Boy's knees and a warm bowl was being pressed to his lips. Sprog smelt vegetables and spices. A peppery . warmth coursed through his icy veins. He choked and asked, quite lucidly, "Where the 'ell did we get soup?"

The bowl was tipped against his mouth several times more. Even when it was empty Sprog still went on clutching at it and eventually it had to be tugged out of his hands. Sprog turned round, saw the Boy's eyes upon him and said, "Hey, mate, you gave me all the blanket. You'll catch your death." Then he tried to lie down and go back to sleep.

But cruel hands got hold of Sprog under his arm pits and wrenched him to his feet! An arm came round his waist like a steel band, holding the blanket in place against him and he was being steered along the tunnel planks. "Leave me be," protested Sprog. "Where we off to *now*?" And then, "I haven't got me duffle bag!"

Sprog tried to struggle free, but he hadn't the strength any more. The Boy was propelling him to the end of the planks, then bearing him on one shoulder down the supports. Out in the open, Sprog felt the snowflakes like icy cobwebs on his face.

It was a journey through a half sleep: broken images, breath-taking cold, moments when Sprog tried to break from the hands which kept him from sleep, others when he yielded with petulant sobs to their obstinate pressure. Fallings over and pickings up, and sometimes a deliberate dive into a white drift where Sprog would find a treacherous bed, a snowy grave.

But it was the dog that led them, scuffling purposefully on as though it, too, had a leader; along one white-clad street, then another, then through a dim alley lit by a single hazy lamp. Next, Sprog was panting up a steep rise to the top of an embankment, along a path open on one side to blinding snow but shut off on the other by a row of tall archways filled in with boards or corrugated iron. The darkness was suddenly rent by a dazzle of blue-green light and a long, massive shape crawled across the sky, spitting sparks.

In the renewed darkness a pinpoint of light shone along the path. The dog hobbled first towards it and then the Boy, with that familiar hesitancy in his approach, trudged on with Sprog clinging to him. There was a singing in Sprog's head and he felt all his senses drifting away again. He *was* falling into a grave, a grave of snow, and the Boy's arms were no longer there trying to hold him back.

The next dream Sprog had was the craziest of all. He was lying in a bed, of sorts, but a bed in some very tall places as full of hollow rumblings as a cave by the sea. A soft, blue light of unknown source filled the cavern of Sprog's fancy with little faces. Eyes were watching Sprog from nooks and crannies in the walls. The small, blue-reflected faces were human, yet not *quite* human. The eyes offered Sprog neither friendliness nor enmity and no voice spoke. A touch of curiosity, perhaps, and Sprog, in his dreamy way, returned their stares with some curiosity of his own.

Not all the faces lacked inquisitiveness, however. Sprog thought he saw another, the faintest of apparitions watching him from somewhere beyond the mysterious blue glow. He could hear breathing — neither the rapid, discordant snuffling of the dog, nor the nasal wheeze of the Boy.

Someone stood there! Sprog wanted to call out to it, "Who are you? What are you staring at me for?" But the words wouldn't come.

Then a figure as light as a ghost drifted across the cave. There was a brief draught of icy air on Sprog's face, as if a door had been opened, then closed — and Sprog, at last, dreamed no more.

Chapter Eight

When Sprog next awoke the fever had left him. His head was clear and the world, or what little bit of it he could see, came rapidly into correct focus. Not that the stuff of his dreams yielded all their secrets; and not that Sprog leapt out of bed at once to embrace them, either. He was too warm, too snug — cocooned in a bedding of a quite astonishing luxuriousness. He felt hungry, of course — as usual — and thirsty and he wanted the toilet, but none of that seemed to matter much.

The place Sprog was in stayed dim and cave-like but now a faint wintry light, coming from somewhere high up, began to cast out most of the shadows. A huge, domed roof curved over Sprog's head and each long wall was fitted with tiers of broad shelves. Sprog's bed had been made up on one bottom shelf and, upon another directly opposite, slept the Boy, but there was no sign of the dog. A tall, cylindrical oil stove was lit between them, glowing a soft blue and giving off enough heat to bake a cake.

The other shelves were mostly packed with long, white boxes, rolls of cloth and bulky plastic bundles. Scattered between, in every position and in some disarray, were dolls. Big dolls, middle-sized dolls and little dolls; dark dolls, fair dolls, black and white dolls — some lying on their backs with eyes closed in a charade of sleep, others sitting against the boxes staring in glassy indifference — no longer the figments of a dream. On a top shelf, close to the curved ceiling, sprawled a huge golliwog, smirking down at Sprog with beady impudence. Here and there, more grotesque still, were scattered bits of dismembered dolls; legs and arms and torsos and heads whose open eyes had perplexed and frightened looks.

What Sprog saw next had him out of bed at the speed of sound. Nearer the back of the arch space was a workbench. A few tools and a couple of dolls' heads had been pushed into a heap and the other end was spread with a table cloth. On the table cloth sat a large packet of cornflakes, a carton of milk and a bowl of sugar. There were two bowls and two spoons. There was an extra plate with slices of bread, covered with a plastic cloth, a butter dish with a lid and an unopened jar of marmalade.

Sprog went across to the Boy and gave him a shake.

"Hey, mate, you been raiding Tesco's?" The Boy hardly stirred. No wonder he was flaked out if he'd spent most of the night laying on this lot!

The dog heard Sprog's voice and crept out from somewhere, licking its chops. It had evidently had a head start on them with breakfast. Sprog opened the milk and gulped half of it down without taking a breath. Then he made himself a marmalade sandwich, thickly buttered. He doubled it over and got his teeth into it. His legs felt stronger already.

Sprog took his breakfast back to bed; his shelf was nearer the door, under a big, semi-circular piece of frosted glass set high in the timber end of the arch. The door was stout, with a brass knob, but when Sprog tried to take a peep outside the door wouldn't open.

Something clicked in Sprog's memory. He munched thoughtfully, trying to piece together the broken fragments of his puzzling night, but they didn't make much sense.

The Boy was sitting up, now, coughing. His bed was made of the same bits and pieces as Sprog's — shabby but thick blankets and strips of coloured hessian borrowed from the shelves. Their pillows were bags filled with cotton waste.

Sprog emptied his mouth and said, "This is a turn up for the book, isn't it, mate? How did we land up here?"

The Boy gave Sprog a slightly sick look, then he went on coughing and lay down again. The dog put his chin on his bed.

Sprog made another marmalade sandwich, put it on a plate and took it over to the Boy, but he seemed to have fallen asleep again, breathing harshly. Sprog took a bite out of the sandwich, then left it on its plate on the bench and went off to do some more exploring, some more thinking.

At the far end of the arch he discovered a closet with an unexpected flush toilet and an old chipped sink fitted with a cold water tap. There was even a strip of frayed but clean towelling hanging on a nail. No . . . the *Boy* had not provided all this!

Sprog doused his face and hands, wiped them on the towelling, then sat at the bench, chin in hands, studying the Boy. The Boy evidently felt the gaze upon him and his eyes flickered open.

Sprog said, accusingly, "You've gone and done it this time, mate — walked us clean into a trap! Dynamite wouldn't shift the lock on that door and there's no way out the back — I've just taken a shufty. Last night . . .

somebody brought us here — right? And now they've shut us in and gone to fetch the Law."

The Boy started coughing again, then reclosed his eyes.

"Don't you fancy a bite of breakfast?" asked Sprog. "There's trouble coming, mate, and I'm not facing it on an empty stomach."

He pulled the cereal bowl towards him. The feel of it in his hands reminded him of something that he couldn't quite remember. He opened the packet of cornflakes, heaped them into the bowl, added milk and sugar and got stuck in.

He was well into his second helping before he said, "They always try to soften you up with fodder, before they start on the old third degree."

The resentment went on mounting inside him. Sprog had always lived on his wits, always got by — as a loner. He didn't fancy having been conned when he was not in his right mind. Made a Patsy of, that's what he'd been!

Then more pieces of the night's jigsaw began to fit. The soup, the mysterious torch flash, the long, agonizing journey through snow . . . but who had led them here and why wasn't the Boy doing his nut about what had happened? The Boy who, at the first breath of another human being, would always make himself scarce . . . become less than a shadow. And how come *this* zany place? Not many things surprised Sprog, but being nicked by a dollmaker was one of them.

A train crawled overhead and the arch was filled with thunder. Its pick-up shoes were still spitting on ice — a blue flash crossed the frosted glass. Sprog grabbed one of the blankets off his bed and slid it further along the shelf, nearer the door. It might be draughty there, but it would be that much easier to make a bolt for it when the trap was sprung.

When the train had gone, the new silence was broken by different sounds; some kids shouting a long way off, the hoot of a tug . . . so they were still near the river? There were sounds much closer; the squeak of heavy wheels, Sprog thought, and not the wheels of a train; a series of soft thuds in snow and . . . the whinnying of a horse? Perhaps he was guessing all wrong, though — a horse and cart didn't make much sense.

The Boy started sitting up again. "Toilet's at the back," said Sprog, but the Boy wasn't going to the toilet. He seemed to be listening for something or someone.

The lock clicked and a wintry draught sped through the arch. Taken unawares, Sprog dived under his shelf. He had a glimpse of two small feet clad in boots with fur round the tops. He hadn't a chance of getting through the door before it was closed and, in any case, his curiosity to see who their visitor was made him incautious enough to stick out his head.

A girl was coming in — backwards — carrying a bulky paper bag in one arm and manoeuvering a cardboard box through the opening with her foot.

She got the stuff in, eventually, gave a furtive peep to and fro along the path outside, then shut the door and turned round. She was wearing a shawl over her head, which she removed, shaking flecks of snow from the ends of long, dark, unkempt hair. She was not especially pretty. Her face was too long and her eyes — brown and gentle — were too big. She had a sallow, sun-starved complexion and a rather prominent, bony chin.

She gave Sprog an unsurprised glance, picked up the

box in her free hand and carried both bundles to the workbench. The mutt went to her at once, snuffling in that puppyish, over-enthusiastic manner it sometimes adopted, and she gave it a pat — as if renewing an acquaintance. Then she went and looked down for quite a long time at the Boy, who had covered his head with a blanket and was feigning sleep.

"Hullo, who are you?" asked Sprog, getting up from the floor.

"Me name's Connie," said the girl. "Connie Angel."

"Mine's Sprog," said Sprog. The girl didn't ask "Sprog what?" She didn't ask anything. She got busy, unpacking the bundles.

Sprog watched her, trying to weigh her up. He had an idea that the girl had pocketed the key after relocking the door. A glance at the keyhole confirmed this — he could see daylight clean through it.

The girl put the things on the workbench. There was a slightly rusty, old-fashioned battery lamp, a tin opener, two chipped enamel mugs and two flat plates, somewhat cracked, with the same blue willow pattern as the mugs had. There was a very tiny, very ancient toy gramophone with a horn, a handle that you wound to keep it going, and three miniature records. There was a bundle of comics done up with an elastic band, and a small pocket torch with a broken glass. Then, out of the cardboard box, came a tin of baked beans, a tin of fruit, another of evaporated milk — and two tins of dog meat! That was the lot.

"Ta," said Sprog.

Connie Angel nodded, face solemn. Then she went back to the Boy and moved the top of his blanket so that she could see his face. He flinched a bit, but let her stroke the rough skin of his cheek with her finger tips. She stood there a long time, saying nothing.

"You get used to his mush after a time," said Sprog. "I suppose you found out he can't talk? We've been together quite a while, but I don't know his name."

The girl let the blanket slip back, then went over to the stove. She gave it a little shake, listening.

"There's enough paraffin in it, for now," she said. "Don't turn it up too high. It smokes."

"Okay," said Sprog. "It *was* you that brought us here, wasn't it?" Connie Angel nodded.

"How did you find us up in that timber stack?" No answer. "Well, ta, anyway. Ta for everything. We'll be on our way soon, when he's had his sleep out." Sprog nodded towards the Boy. "He was up all night, you know, looking after me. I been sick or something. Was it you give us the soup?"

"Yes," said Connie Angel.

"It was nice soup," said Sprog. He laughed awkwardly. "I thought you was going to bring the coppers."

Connie Angel looked at Sprog as if he had told her a riddle she didn't quite understand.

"Funny place, this," went on Sprog. "All them dolls . . . give me the creeps last night."

Connie Angel said, "You'll be all right, here. Nobody will bother you, if you stay quiet. Keep the gramophone down and cover the food up — we get rats along here, sometimes." She glanced back at the Boy's bed. "He looks very flushed. Make him stay in bed. I'll call in here again later — after school."

"Sunday school?" asked Sprog.

Connie Angel's brown eyes were puzzled. "It's Monday," she said. That shook Sprog! The last he remembered, it had been Saturday night. That meant they'd spent *two* nights in the timber stack, with a whole day sandwiched between. He must have caught sleeping sickness!

Connie Angel went out into the snow. When Sprog tried out the handle he found that the door was locked again. The dog sat there, whining softly, then it went off to a dark corner and wet against the wall.

Sprog didn't worry too much — did not try to kick the door down or yell after the girl. If he really wanted to escape, he reckoned he could manage it. (He did not bother to work out how.) Meanwhile, Sprog thought, they had it made; warm stove, more food than he'd seen in weeks and beds you could kip in without biting your tongue to stop your teeth chattering, or crawling about in the middle of the night to dodge a puddle.

Every time Sprog looked at the nest of blankets on his shelf he yawned and wanted to crawl back. If the coppers arrived, they could carry him off, bed and all, and he wouldn't even trouble to open his eyes.

The Boy slept on, gradually becoming more restless. Several times Sprog had to pick up one of his blankets and tuck it about his shoulders. He didn't much like the sound of his breathing — his cold must have got a lot worse.

Sprog opened a tin of baked beans and warmed them on the oil heater. While they were cooking he tried out the gramophone. A crusty nursery rhyme squeaked through the horn and Sprog let it play itself out, but didn't bother to turn over the record. He went to bed instead, after one spoonful of beans.

He must have slept undisturbed for several hours,

until the whine of the dog awakened him. It was pawing at the door, restless to get out. What did it want — its new playmate, the girl? They seemed to have taken a fancy to each other. Sprog guessed, then, that it had probably been the mutt which had led her to the timber stack that night — just as once, long ago, it had lured Sprog to the Boy, and wanted him to stay. The girl had followed the dog, found the boys, and brought them here. Only it was the Boy and his mutt she really fancied; she'd more or less treated Sprog like something the cat had brought in!

Sprog got up, still yawning, spooned cold beans on to a plate, ate some and took the rest to the Boy. He thought he was awake, but his sitting up and wild looking round was evidently only part of a nightmare. The puckered skin of his face had a tight, shiny look and when Sprog put his hand against the rough cheek, it burned hot and there was no sweat. Sprog tried giving him milk instead, but he spat it out.

The dog forgot the girl, left off scraping at the locked door, and laid its head forlornly at the Boy's feet. The Boy calmed a little and fell back into a kind of sleep.

Time dragged on but Connie Angel did not come back. Trains thundered by at regular intervals, a little faster now, with less sizzling of their shoes as if the snow was beginning to clear on the rails.

Eventually the stove went out and an all too familiar cold crept stealthily through the arch. Sprog opened a tin of dog's meat and put it in the thick enamel dish that Connie had left for the mutt near the closet. Then he came back and laid an extra blanket over the Boy and wrapped another round his own shoulders. The bread was going stale. Sprog buttered a slice and thought of opening the tin of fruit, but he didn't fancy it. In the end he just sat on the stool by the workbench, head in hands, watching the Boy.

The Boy sat up. His head and shoulders seemed to have shrunk and he looked as stiff and spindly as a wooden doll. His eyes were staring into some world of terror that was all his own. It was as though for a single instant, in a unique flash of recognition, the Boy took Sprog into the edge of his mysterious and far off world.

Then he spoke! What came out of the thin, scarred mouth, were not the mere random mutterings of someone in a delirium, but words and phrases, quietly and sensibly spoken; the rise and fall of cadence, words having true meaning and the intent to communicate. The feverish eyes remained fixed intelligently on Sprog, and then the voice paused, as if inviting Sprog to reply. Yet . . . the speech was so strange that it might have been uttered by a visitor from a different planet.

Sprog jerked to his feet. "What was that, mate? What was you trying to say?"

But Sprog was too late; the Boy's eyes were again lost in mist. Very slowly the lashless lids closed, then he lay down, one arm flung over his pillow, and for a time he slept and was still.

Chapter Nine

When Connie Angel arrived she carried a tin of paraffin and another bulging paper carrier bag. She glanced at Sprog, then began unloading her cargo on to the work bench.

"Glad you showed up," said Sprog. "Getting a bit nippy in here. Can I fill up the stove?"

"If you know how."

"Of course I know how." Sprog got the stove going and warmed his hands. By then, Connie Angel had finished unpacking. There were some apples, another tin of dog's meat, some bread rolls and a clock. It was a small ornate, mantlepiece clock with a pair of rampant lions holding up a round gold face in Roman numerals. The glass was cracked and the slightly bent hands pointed at approximately a quarter to five.

"Is that the right time?" asked Sprog.

"Near enough," said Connie Angel.

"Ta, it's a nice clock." He looked quizzically at Connie. "Where do you get hold of all this stuff?"

Connie Angel didn't answer. She took her soft, brown, dreamy gaze over to the Boy's bed. She moved the top of the blanket and felt his face.

Sprog said, "He took very queer a while ago. He got me quite scared. You know what, though? He talked, only it was in a funny sort of lingo. I never thought of it before, but you know what I think? He's a ruddy foreigner! With a mush like that, he could be an Eskimo or something, couldn't he?"

Sprog's speculations did not seem to interest Connie Angel. She tucked the blankets closer around the Boy's shoulders. The dog looked on, its eyes filled with a wet sadness.

"It's 'flu, I expect," said Connie Angel. "He sat up in that timber stack for hours, with nothing to cover him, and on the telly they said it was the coldest night for ten years."

"You're not kidding!" said Sprog. "I got the 'flu an' all, you know. A touch of. I soon got over it, so I expect he will too. We're tough, him and me."

"We've got some medicine at home," said Connie Angel. "I'll run and fetch it."

"I'll come with you," said Sprog, glancing at the big key in Connie's hand.

"No."

"You don't have to keep locking us in," said Sprog.

"If the door's left," said Connie Angel, "somebody might come in. We get all sorts, along here." She let the key drop back into her pocket.

The dog got up, snuffled at Connie's legs, then went off on the prowl. Sprog said, "The mutt ought to be let out, sometimes. It's not very nice, having a dog shut in here all day."

Connie Angel gave Sprog a more intent look than usual, then went out, locking the door, of course.

She was back two trains later. By then the piece of frosted glass had gown dark and Sprog had tried out the new battery lamp, putting it on the bench behind the paraffin can so that it wouldn't shine on the Boy's face.

Sprog looked up from his elbows. "You don't live all

that far away then?"

She went straight for the Boy's bed, picking up a spoon on the way and looking to see if it was clean. Sprog watched, hands in pockets, while she tipped medicine out of a bottle into the spoon, held up the Boy's head and got the stuff down his throat. The Boy choked and opened his eyes. There was a touch of his old terror when he saw the face above him, but when Connie let go his head flopped back on to the pillow and he sighed back to sleep.

Sprog asked, "How do you know it's the right sort of stuff?"

"It's only cough medicine," shrugged Connie. "Can you read?"

" 'Course I can read!"

"The directions on the bottle say, 'Shake well, one teaspoonful every four hours.' I'll leave the bottle here."

She got up and began drawing something out of her coat pocket. She made juicy noises with her lips and the dog came running, or, if not exactly running, limping skittishly out of a corner and licking Connie's hand. It was in for a big surprise!

Connie Angel put a collar round its neck — there was already a lead attached. The collar was oversized and spikey with metal studs. The mutt just stood there, looking baffled, ears laid back flat, tail between its legs and if Connie Angel had tried to dress it in a pink nightie it couldn't have looked more stupid. It turned round two or three times, trying to shake off the collar, practically falling over its three good legs.

Sprog laughed. "You'll never get that to walk along on a lead. He won't know if you're pushing or pulling!"

Connie Angel made for the door, dragging the mutt

with her. It looked as if it was off to its execution.

When she turned the key, Sprog said, "Wouldn't mind a bit of exercise myself." Connie Angel didn't take the hint. "What happens if the bloke who runs this place calls in for a couple of dolls' heads?"

Connie said, "He won't. He's old and ill and he hasn't been able to work for weeks. That's why I've been keeping an eye on his shop. There's a card out here, nailed to the door, and it says that the business is closed down indefinitely. Satisfied?"

The lock clicked.

Sprog got his supper and read a comic. The Boy woke up much too early for his next dose of Connie Angel's medicine, but as he started coughing Sprog thought he might as well give him some of it. Sprog got half a spoonful down the Boy's throat and the other half down his chin. He thought he was looking round for his dog, but, after staring into the gloom once or twice with his feverish eyes, he went back to sleep.

A little later on, Sprog checked the stove, switched off the electric lamp and got into bed, not bothering to take off his clothes.

He wondered if Connie Angel had taken the mutt home for the night, but just as he was dozing off he felt a draught from the door and the dog snuffled in, shaking itself and crawling off to sleep. Connie Angel did not come in with it. The door was locked again and faint footsteps died away outside.

A train woke Sprog. A dusty shaft of moonlight came through the frosted glass. Sprog had taken the little broken torch to bed with him and put the clock on the stool. He shone the torch at the clock. Half past six.

Something stirred in the shadows of the shelves, and Sprog swivelled the torch beam.

Dog and Boy were awake. What was more, the Boy had got out of bed and was putting on his anorak. He was stooped over his bed, stuffing things into his háversack. The dog sat waiting beside him. Either the Boy was sleep walking, or Connie Angel's medicine was a miracle cure.

"Where are you off to, mate?" asked Sprog.

The Boy finished stuffing things into his bag and did up the buckles. He put it on his shoulder and loped towards the door, the dog at his heels. He tried the handle.

Sprog said, "That'll get you nowhere very fast, mate."

The Boy twisted the handle again, then tried to jerk the door to and fro. When he turned round there was a touch of panic.

"Relax," said Sprog. "You don't want to go out there in the snow. You've been sick, see? Don't you remember?"

In the torchlight the Boy's shoulders were drooped and dejected. He gave up trying to batter the door down and came back slowly, sitting on his shelf. The dog was wagging its tail and gladly nuzzling its nose into the Boy's hands as if he had just walked back from the dead.

"I know how you feel," said Sprog. "But what's the hurry? We're all right, here. We've never had it so good. It'll be breakfast in bed next. Fancy some cornflakes? Milk's a bit off, but I expect that girl will bring us some more. She may be a bit queer upstairs, but when it comes to delivering the necessary she's better than a ruddy freight train."

They stayed put and Sprog lost count of the days. They were not many, but each felt like a month. The trains passed overhead like the broken chimes of a clock and sometimes the vibrations of their wheels would send one of the dolls toppling from its shelf and Sprog would stick it back.

From the little that Sprog could see, the winter still blasted across the outer world. Winds battered at the door and made the stove flicker; snow built up against the boarded front of the arch, followed by icy rain which tried to wash it away and leaked in through the frosted glass.

Despite their rapid recovery after their ordeal, neither of the boys was fit enough, yet, to undergo any more exposure. There was also neither the opportunity nor the need to pilfer; so they got themselves forgotten by shop keepers and those early, vigilant guardians of milk floats — and they were probably half crossed off in policemen's note books.

Twice a day, at around half past eight in the morning and soon after four in the afternoon, Sprog got the fidgety feeling that they were being watched, though he could never quite catch an eye on the other side of the keyhole.

It was at these times that Connie Angel arrived, never empty handed. More tins of food, extra clothing a reasonable fit for one or other of the boys, and more and more junk of varying usefulness; a vase of artificial roses, more comics, more scratched records, tatty books with unreadable titles, and a game of snakes and ladders with buttons for counters.

Very regularly she came, unpacked her goods, dragged the mutt off for a short walk at the end of its tether, then cooked them breakfast, deftly breaking eggs and jiggling the pan over the stove. Then she'd scoop the slightly sooty food on to two plates and turn her soft, serious brown eyes on the Boy when they began to eat.

She'd feed the dog a tin of meat, or something she'd brought in a newspaper parcel. Connie would spoon the stuff into the enamel dish, but if there was something she could hold in her fingers she would tempt the dog with it, making those juicy noises with her lips until the mutt came and took it out of her hand.

The first time this happened the Boy stopped eating and watched his dog take the food out of Connie's hand. When she had gone, he held a biscuit in his fingers and waited for the dog to come and fetch it. The mutt wouldn't play.

"Well, it's had its breakfast, hasn't it?" said Sprog. "And you don't want to let her needle you, mate. So she's good with animals, that's all. You don't reckon she's going to take your mutt away from you?"

The Boy threw the biscuit away across the arch, and the dog perversely pounced on it as though it was the first bite in a month. The Boy looked sullen.

Early on Friday morning — or perhaps it was Saturday — Sprog saw a flicker of sunlight on the frosted glass. For Sprog it was like the first touch of spring and the sap rose as though there were buds sprouting out of his ears.

Connie Angel arrived as usual, put her carrier bag on the bench, then took the dog out for its constitutional.

After five minutes she unlocked the door and came back in, took off her top coat and hung it on the antique hat stand she had dragged there the day before.

Sprog said, "Got any more games at home? We're getting a bit tired of snakes and ladders."

"I'll have a look," said Connie.

"Do we get any time off for good behaviour?" asked Sprog.

"What do you mean?"

"Just a joke," shrugged Sprog. "Seriously, though, we're okay now, the Boy and me. Ta for everything, but we'll be off soon — if it's all the same to you."

Connie Angel looked hurt. "I'm not stopping you, if that's what you want. I thought you wanted somewhere — a sort of home, like." She glanced anxiously at the Boy, as if seeking his opinion, but the Boy stared dumbly back.

Sprog went on, "Yeah, it's been very nice. It's not that we don't appreciate it, but this locking up lark . . . there's a lot of world outside, and we'd like a shufty at it, now and then."

Connie's eyes dwelt on him thoughtfully. "If you go out you'll only get yourselves into trouble again. And it's still ever so cold. I thought you'd had enough of being out on your own, with nowhere to go."

"Yeah," said Sprog. "I'm not saying we want to push off altogether. Just go in and out, like. If *we* had a key . . ."

"There's only one," said Connie Angel. "Besides, you'd be seen and then we'd all be in trouble. I — I shouldn't have let you use this place, really. If Mr Hopkins found out . . . "

"Who's he?"

"The old man who rents the arch. It's the railway that actually owns it."

"Yeah, I see you got problems," said Sprog.

"We'll think of something," said Connie Angel, solemnly.

"When?" asked Sprog.

But Connie Angel had got to the end of her bit of the conversation. She fried some fresh bacon, flinching as a speck of fat spat on her wrist. Sprog hovered innocently, first pretending to help Connie get the breakfast, making his bed — with his back to the door. Connie dished up their breakfast and fed the dog. When she had done all that she slipped her coat on and started doing up the buttons. She slid her long, thin hands into the pockets. After some fumbling and thinking her eyes dropped to the floor at the foot of the hatstand.

"Lost something?" asked Sprog.

Connie Angel gave his face a sharp look of suspicion. "My key!"

Sprog looked under his chair, then shifted the plates about on the tablecloth. "Perhaps you dropped it in the snow outside," he said.

"There isn't any snow outside," said Connie Angel. She worked it out carefully for a minute, then added, "Anyway, if I locked the door when I came in, the key couldn't be out there, could it?"

"Not unless it fell through the letter box," said Sprog.

"There *isn't* a letter box."

"P'raps you never locked the door."

Connie Angel went over and turned the handle. The door opened.

"Told you so," said Sprog. "Not to worry. We'll prop it up from the inside, see? When you come again, knock three times and we'll know it's you and not an undesirable."

Connie Angel bit her lip. It was hard to tell whether she was merely puzzled — or hurt.

When she had left, Sprog flipped the key out of his pocket and laughed. "Easy!" he said. "That puts her in her place, don't it mate? I'm going for a scout round after breakfast, okay?"

Not the Boy, though. He sat on his stool, nibbling, eyes still big and haunted with his sickness, gaze patiently on the high window as if already watching for the first star.

Chapter Ten

Among the items of clothing which Connie Angel had brought along was a jacket Sprog had taken an immediate fancy to. It was shiny-black with a zip front, two pairs of pockets and a trim of fur round the collar. Sprog put this on, turned the key and let the mongrel follow him.

Outside he took a couple of sweet, deep breaths and a cautious glance in each direction. The path, clear of snow now, ran along the top of an embankment past the railway arches until it became a road on the other side of some white posts, turning a corner under a bridge.

At the bottom of the bank was a large and desolate waste, dumpy with mounds of rubbish and scattered with derelict chassis and loose tyres. The dog, free at last of Connie Angel's tow rope, scampered down the grassy slope. Nobody was about, so Sprog followed, his legs still shaky, the cloudy sky dazzling, the world suddenly wide and free. There were familiar sounds from the river concealed behind big, square grey buildings across a rusty wire fence. The dinosaur's neck of a crane peered gigantically between two roofs, and a block of marble flats with balconies loomed with more windows than a fly has eyes.

Sprog's imagination traced a route along the wire fence, dwelling as usual upon a possible emergency escape route. There would be a gap in the fence somewhere — there nearly always was — and on the other side, a fast exit into a maze of riverside streets and alleys. Sprog documented the information at the back of his mind and, seeing nothing much else of interest, whistled the mutt.

But the dog never obeyed a call unless it suited its convenience. It had limped off towards one corner of the waste ground and all Sprog could see was its brown tail waving like something growing out of the long grass. The mongrel was rooting about in a dip, probably sniffing at an old boot. The depression in the ground, not far from one stretch of fence, was deep and foul. In trying to get near enough to the dog to yank it out, Sprog discovered a small wooden shed on the lip of the weed infested depression. He hadn't noticed it at first because it had been virtually swallowed by a riotous growth of weeds and brambles.

Sprog wasn't especially interested except that the very existence of such a place was irresistible. Careful not to snag his jacket, he found the door. There was a small padlock, green with age and too corroded to pick. Sprog examined the screws holding the hasp: there were three, not very big, one of which had a broken head. Sprog had soon prised them out using his fingers and a piece of wood as a lever. He pushed the door in and it creaked stiffly into a stinking darkness. When his eyes adjusted to the dimness Sprog saw that the timber floor was broken through in places and underneath the soil was dust-dry and sterile. But the dog smelt life in it. Nosing its way through splintered boards it darted away like a mongoose after a snake. A rat? Sprog eventually got hold of the mutt by its middle and dragged it out. It whined softly, reluctant to leave, and went off to sniff again in the dip. Sprog pushed the shed door to and put the screws back. He brushed himself down and, his eyes thoughtfully measuring the distance across the deserted waste, climbed back to the railway path, leaving the dog to follow.

Sprog wandered along the faces of the arches. The enclosed fronts had names printed over them — dealers, storage firms and the like. At the bridge a train crawled overhead, held up by a wintry red signal. A small girl leaned out of a window and waved at Sprog and Sprog waved back. The train dragged itself off.

The second arch after the road bridge had a dusty window on each side of an inset door. Sprog peeped through one of the windows and saw the white face of a grandfather clock staring out of a dim clutter of furniture. Then, before he could dive out of sight, a horse's hooves clip-clopped on the road, a cart swung out from beneath the railway bridge and came to a slithering halt.

The horse snorted and a man climbed down from the front seat. He was a very tall, thin man with a bony frame and long, thin clothes and a sallow, graveyard face. His large, brown eyes settled briefly on Sprog. He felt for a key, unlocked the door, then swung the whole face of the arch up and over. Sprog had a glimpse of furniture and shelves of crockery crowded back at each side to leave a broad avenue between. The man climbed back in his seat, gave the reins a jerk and, holding his hat and ducking his head, drove the horse and cart right in, with inches to spare.

Sprog stayed put because he was interested — much more interested than scared. He had just read what was printed in painted letters on the side of the cart — and there was more or less the same information on the arch itself:

BERT ANGEL

Antiques Second hand goods
Brass and Iron

The man squeezed slowly between the furniture and the side of the cart and came to the back. He saw that Sprog was still standing there.

Sprog said, "I was just looking at the big clock in the window. It's a nice clock."

"You mean, you and me are going to do a little business?"

"I was only looking," said Sprog. "Are you Mister Angel himself?"

The man nodded and took a bag of sweets out of his pocket. He put one in his mouth and sucked. He went on sucking unhurriedly, his slow, brown gaze taking in the dog. Then he handed the bag of sweets to Sprog.

"Ta," said Sprog, taking a sweet.

Bert Angel squeezed back into the arch and began heaving some of the bits of furniture on to the cart.

"Can I go and pat your horse?" asked Sprog.

"If you're going to stick around," said Bert Angel, "you can make yourself useful. If you was to get in the cart, I could hand you up some of the small things."

"How much?"

"How much what?"

"For helping to load the cart?"

"Say five pence, if you stack it careful," said Bert Angel. I'm not what you'd call a mean man, myself."

Sprog took off his jacket and hung it on the tailboard. Then he cocked a leg over and Bert gave him a number of articles to pack in odd corners: a brass

89

fender, some crockery, this and that. Sprog didn't break anything but he had to move fast to keep up with Bert Angel.

"That's the lot, then," said Bert, at last. He fished a coin out of his pocket and spun it at Sprog.

"Ta," said Sprog. He whistled for the dog and started putting on his jacket. Bert Angel was looking at the jacket.

"That's smart gear you've got there," he said. "Continental styling — very natty indeed."

"It's a nice jacket," agreed Sprog.

Bert Angel's eyes held a slightly amused expression as he handed out the bag of sweets again. Then he said, "High class, second-hand clothes is part of my trade. I've got an eye for a good cut of cloth. I'd ask where you got hold of it — only I'm a man of no curiosity, myself."

The arch door was locked so Sprog tapped the secret signal which had, by now, sounded on a dozen different doors, in a dozen different places. The Boy let him in, and the mutt, then went back to bed.

Sprog sat on his own bit of shelf, not saying anything at first. He played with the 5p piece Bert Angel had given him, thoughtfully flipping it several times. Then he told the Boy, "I've taken a good shufty round, mate. Snow's cleared and there's nobody much about. You know what, though? I met Connie Angel's old man. He's a junk merchant. No wonder she got hold of all this stuff. They've got a shop place in one of these arches. I knew who he was even before I saw the name — they're the spitting image, him and Connie. Come to that, you could hardly tell any of *them* apart — Connie, the old man or their horse." Sprog laughed.

He went over to the workbench and helped himself to some food. He sat on a stool, saw that the Boy's eyes were still open and went on, "I been thinking. If we had to scarper some time, on the quick, we wouldn't want to leave everything behind. What we want, mate, is a panic kit. A few tins of food, clothes and that, stuffed in a bag and stashed away where we could collect it on the way out — in case of fire, sort of. And I've found just the place, this shed not far off. It's got a nice dry place under the floor, and we could hide some gear in it. All we'd have to do is grab it on the way out and we'd be away so fast they couldn't catch us with ruddy greyhounds." The Boy seemed to listen.

Sprog went on, more awkwardly, not sure how the Boy felt: "Maybe we could have two bags, one for you and one for me — in case one of us wanted to scarper and the other didn't." He was remembering how he used to feel: not wanting to crowd the Boy, not making him think Sprog couldn't get by without him, or the other way round.

They all slept for a while until the light began to dim in the frosted glass and the dolls vanished one by one into shadows.

There came three knocks on the door. Sprog got up and let Connie Angel in. Her hair was straggly with new rain as, without a word, she carried out her usual delivery service at the workbench. Nothing fancy this time — only tins of food and a bag of eggs.

The Boy paid no attention — not even when she fed his mutt. Connie sat on a stool waiting for the dog to lick the dish clean. Then she said, "I wonder if it ever had a name? Everybody should have a name."

"What's your horse's name?" asked Sprog.

"Nellie . . . " said Connie Angel. It was a full quarter minute before she thought out the implications and gave Sprog her solemn, hurt look, her eyes full of questions she didn't voice.

She was gone soon afterwards, letting herself out and apparently forgetting to take the dog for its walk. Sprog guessed that she'd come there straight from school. When she got home, wherever that was, her father Bert might give her hell — over the jacket and everything else — and there could be trouble. Despite the junk man's friendliness, which might have been a blind to keep Sprog from making a bolt for it too soon. Sprog was too old a hand not to wish there was a second way out of the arch.

As soon as Sprog switched on the battery lamp the Boy put on wellingtons, anorak and woollen cap, gave Sprog a glance which was some kind of cheerio, then went out with his dog. Sprog locked the door from the inside and got busy.

There were two big waterproof bags which Connie Angel had left behind. One was navy blue, the other dark green. Sprog chose the blue — he must remember to tell the Boy which was which.

He packed each of them with tins of corned beef, fruit and baked beans. Between them he wedged rolled up socks, woollen jumpers and pairs of shoes. There was still room, so he added apples and oranges — and a tin of dog's meat to the Boy's bag. Torches, two tins of shandy, two string vests, then his old anorak and odd wellingtons. He tied the necks of the bags with string and carried them over to the door. He opened the door and poked his head out, listening; then, carrying a bag under each arm, he heeled the door shut and set off down the darkening embankment.

Sprog hid the bags under the broken floor boards of the shed beside the dip, hoping that whatever the mutt had been sniffing after wouldn't nibble in and set up home in his change of laundry.

Chapter Eleven

When Saturday morning came round again Connie's faintly hesitant knock at the arch door found Sprog only just yawning awake. It was still dark and a swift on-and-off click of his torch showed that the Boy was not yet home.

Sprog unlocked the door. He didn't bother to turn the key afterwards, but he didn't leave it in the lock, either.

"Couldn't you sleep?" he asked Connie, not getting an answer.

Connie Angel placed a carrier bag on the bench, her slow, competent hands getting out bags and tins.

"I reckon you could keep an army going," said Sprog. "Does your old man know you're lifting all this stuff?"

Connie's eyes were like those of a mother cat who knew exactly which of her kittens had stolen the cream out of the pantry.

"Pardon?" she asked. Then she gave up pretending she didn't know that Sprog had not only stolen the key but made a visit to Bert Angel's shop. She went on in a dreamy monotone, "I keep house for my dad. I haven't got a mum. We get things cheap at the market, because we have a stall there on Wednesdays. Do you want your breakfast?"

"Ta," said Sprog. He suddenly wanted to stop teasing Connie Angel, but wasn't sure how to go about it.

"Fried egg on toast?"

"If that's an egg cup I see you just brought," said Sprog, "I wouldn't mind it boiled for a change, if it's all the same to you. Not too hard boiled and have you got any salt?"

Connie nodded. They waited for the egg to boil in a small, battered saucepan. A throbbing train shook a little Swiss doll off her shelf. She nearly fell into the saucepan and Connie picked her up and thrust her back. Connie Angel never showed much interest in the dolls.

"Will *he* be back soon?" she asked, meaning the Boy. Her voice held just a touch of anxiety.

"You tell me," shrugged Sprog. "He likes the night — he always did. Him and his mutt! Anyway, they won't stop out when it gets light." He poured out some cornflakes and changed the subject. "I got on all right with your old man. Does he know about . . . the Boy and me?" The light from the little lamp was candle-soft and it was hard to read Connie's face by it.

"I reckon he spotted that jacket you give me."

"It doesn't matter," said Connie Angel. She pushed the egg across. Sprog smashed in the top with his spoon.

"That's a nice horse you got."

Connie's eyes brightened. "Mare, not horse. I'm getting her breakfast in a minute. Fancy coming along to help?"

Sprog hesitated. "Okay, only I don't know much about horses — I mean, mares. I'll follow you along a bit later, all right?"

"Don't be too long, then," said Connie. "We always make an early start on Saturdays." With her hand on the door knob she turned and added, "It was my dad said you could come."

She must almost have bumped into the Boy, except that nobody ever quite managed that, for he opened the door and crept in as soon as she had gone. From his neat appearance he might have spent the night in a three-star hotel, with showers; the dog, however, had apparently made do with some cosy nook between a manure heap and a stack of wet coal.

The Boy had a bottle of milk under his anorak and a couple of eggs in his pocket. He put them on the bench and stared for a moment at the fresh supplies Connie had brought.

"We don't have to go raiding milk carts no more, mate," said Sprog.

The Boy's look back this time was a shade remote — perhaps sullen. Sprog went to the closet and had a wash. There was a soap dish there, now, with a new tablet of soap in it. He dragged a broken comb through his tangled hair, slipped on a pair of brown shoes Connie had brought, then zipped up his continental jacket.

The Boy was drinking milk — out of his stolen bottle, not Connie's carton. Sprog threw him the keys.

"See you, then. Look after me kit and that. I'm not taking the duffle bag this trip."

He stepped out into the morning. The railway path was tacky under foot, but the sky was clear and studded with late stars.

Nellie had a stall deep in the Angels' arch which was lit with a dusty, dangling electric light bulb. Connie was fitting harness to the mare. Nellie gave Sprog a wary glance over her nosebag and shuffled her hooves.

The cart stood by itself, shaft tips resting on the floor. Bert Angel was curled over a little desk with pigeon holes, looking through a book covered with spidery writing. He hardly seemed to notice Sprog until he handed him a card from the top of a pile.

"We do the round on Saturdays — want to lend a hand? We cover one district at a time and we plan it like a battle. Connie goes ahead on her bike and pushes these cards through letter boxes. That way, people know we're coming and they've got time to peek in their attics, or decide whether it's an opportune moment to get rid of that old piano in their parlour."

The card was neatly printed but with nothing fancy:

BERT ANGEL
Specialist in Antiques
Good Prices Paid for Second Hand Furniture,
Brass, Copper, etc, etc
Our Representative Will Call Today.

"You can always do with some help in an expanding business," went on Bert Angel. "I'm getting a bit past it, jumping up and down off that cart, collecting stuff." He gave Sprog a boiled sweet and looked at him shrewdly. "The rate's ten pence an hour and a bonus if you pick up anything good. What do you say?"

"You're on," said Sprog.

"That's the ticket," said Bert Angel. "I like a lad with a bit of initiative, myself."

Connie finished with Nellie, came and collected the cards and pushed her bike out of the arch. Bert Angel took his time about harnessing the mare between the shafts. He talked a lot, compared with Connie Angel:

"If it wasn't for Connie, I reckon I'd have gone in for a lorry by now. She thinks the world of this old nag, does Connie. Mind you, Nellie's cheaper than any lorry. She don't need petrol and she don't need tax and she don't need new tyres." He handed Sprog a huge oil can. "Give the hubs a touch of this, my lad. You'll see the holes."

Sprog oiled all the wheels and, by the time that was done, Bert Angel was handing the sweets round again.

He leaned against one of his wardrobes and went on, "I'm a man of no great ambition, myself, but there's something about junk, you know. Creative, that's what junk is. Somebody has no use for an old clock, say, and I happen to know a party who lies awake at nights dreaming of owning one just like it. Who's the man between? Who's the one that brings both parties together in peace and satisfaction? Bert Angel! Well, Connie's had a good start. Let's hit the road."

Bert Angel got up on the high seat and Sprog climbed up with him. Bert gave a little tug at the reins and made clicking noises with his mouth and Nellie carefully pushed the cart backwards out of the arch. Then Bert Angel got her going forwards and she pulled them along the narrow road, round under the railway bridge and into the streets.

Bert Angel looked slyly at Sprog. "How does it feel up here?" he asked.

"Okay," said Sprog.

A policeman on his beat turned the corner. Bert Angel waved to him and he waved back with a smile and took no further notice of them.

Bert Angel gave Sprog that sidelong glance again. "You feeling seasick or anything?"

"Who, me?" said Sprog.

"You can always hide down in the cart, if you

fancy." But Sprog stayed where he was. Next time they met a copper, *he'd* wave too!

Bert pulled up at a corner. "This is where we get started, then. You knock on all the doors, but only once, mind. When you get an answer, all you have to say is that you're from Bert Angel. They may give you a snooty look, but you just be courteous, see? Courtesy is important in our business. If the party slams a door in your face, mind you don't get your nose caught in it. And if a client has something for sale, I'll tell you how much to offer. You may find things left outside the door for free, only watch it. I knew a geezer, once, who helped himself to an old pram — only there happened to be a baby in it and he nearly got charged with kidnapping."

They plied their trade all morning and at the end of it the cart was half full: tables, chairs, a roll top desk, three different mirrors, two old radios and a TV set, several brass ornaments, a bronze fender and a double bed spring.

"Not bad — not bad at all," said Bert Angel. His brown eyes resting on Sprog had a new and warmer expression. "What did you do — charm the birds off the trees? I reckon you've got the touch. That's what we need in this business — the *touch*. We done it all respectable and quiet, too. I never was one for hollering and ringing bells, myself. Want to come back and help unload?"

"Ta," said Sprog. He felt a funny tingle all over, as if his undersized body had started to grow at last — just a little. The twitch of a muscle here, a muscle there; the broadening of rib and tightening of bone.

A shaft of wintry sunshine had brought the kids out,

like a swarm of early bees, to play with the abandoned vehicles on the waste ground.

Driving past, Bert Angel said, "Last year a family of foxes set up house over there under some old shed. Connie went across, of course, and tried to coax the vixen out. Not even my Connie could get a fox to eat out of her hand, but she used to leave them food. Connie would feed a rattle snake if she thought it was hungry."

Connie was waiting for them when they got back. She helped them unload the cart, then unhitched Nellie and took her back to her stall. Bert Angel carefully counted out Sprog's wages, then he said, "If there's some little thing you fancy, help yourself. You've earned it."

Sprog knew what he wanted at once. "Can I have one of them looking glasses?"

"Take your pick," said Bert Angel.

Sprog chose the mirror with a gold frame. It had a little stand and when he looked at his face in it, the old, dark glass reflected back an old, dark face — which rather pleased him. Bert and Connie both stood watching Sprog look at himself in the mirror. Sprog couldn't tell what they were thinking.

Sprog wanted to tell them, look, I'm not what you think. I'm not just a kid who came along to help on Saturday morning. I'm a runaway, a tearaway, and if you had any sense, you'd hand me over. You might even collect yourself a reward!

They were a mystery, those Angels. Taking him for granted, knowing things about him that he hadn't even tried to tell; trusting him, treating him ordinary, without questions, without expecting him to be in any way different. To them he was just Sprog and neither of them had ever asked, Sprog *what*?

Bert Angel said, "Well, any time you want a job, you come and see me. If I'm not here I'll be out on my round, or at the market, or at home. Twenty-nine Beak Street. It's just on the other side of the railway. Remember that? Twenty-nine Beak Street."

"Ta, a lot," said Sprog, and he couldn't say any more. He turned away and walked off along the railway path. On the way, out of old habit, he glanced back over his shoulder, but Bert Angel was not watching to see where he went.

Sprog didn't go straight home to the arch. Clutching the looking glass under his arm, he cut back through the railway bridge and found a sweet shop. He spent one of his 10p pieces on a bag of assorted toffees. The Boy ate toffees sometimes. He also bought himself a brand new comic with a free gift inside and then he came back under the railway bridge and went home.

The door was locked and Sprog had to wait to be let in. He swaggered in, locking the door behind him, still glowing deep inside with self-discovery as bright as a seam of gold. Together they had crawled through a long tunnel, in the dark, often clinging together in the winter's embrace; but now, for Sprog, there had arrived a moment when there beckoned a far-off spring. Could the Boy not share *that*, too?

The Boy returned to his bed. He crouched forward, gripping the sides of the shelf with his hands, staring at Sprog, staring at what nestled under his arm. Sprog knew that something was wrong. Instinctively, he glanced at the dog as if the better to understand the Boy's mood. And the dog lurked indecisively between them, ears back, warning Sprog — but Sprog didn't understand. He propped the mirror on the bench with the glass turned so that when he sat beside the Boy it reflected a dark image of them both.

"Nice, isn't it?" said Sprog, gabbling on: "I got it for going on a junk round with Bert Angel. We waved to a copper, and here's the laugh — he flipping waved back! I made fifty pence and half of it's for you and I bought you some sweets." Sprog threw the packet beside the Boy, but he didn't look at it.

"Them Angels are okay. I reckon they've known about us for a long time, but they never let on. What did I tell you, mate? We've got it made. No more thieving, no more running from coppers, no more sleeping in bleeding sewers."

But the Boy was looking at him like a frightened cat, recoiling, his damaged face doubly disfigured with inexplicable hate. He left his bed; he loped to the bench and stood in front of the looking glass for a moment, his blunt face mirrored darkly. A sound of sorts rattled in his throat, then he swung back his arm and smashed at the hated glass with his fist, sending fragments glittering across the stone floor.

Out of the awful silence, Sprog said, "You've busted me mirror! I only wanted to comb me hair."

The Boy's knuckles bled and bled, but he showed no sign of pain.

Chapter Twelve

Sprog had half forgotten that he was a fugitive. He covered the short distance to Bert Angel's arch open and unafraid, hands in pockets, whistling as if all the world knew him — knew him as Sprog, Bert Angel's representative. In the streets under the bridge, ladies had begun to smile at him across washed doorsteps, listen amusedly to his perky chatter, reading no secrets in the freckled face with its snub-nosed, unfrightened candour.

Connie's gift of the jacket awakened in Sprog a latent taste for clothes. Today he wore a smart pair of creased trousers, a pair of brown suede shoes, a brightly coloured shirt and a speckled bow tie. Even his straw-coloured hair had a new style — it was combed!

Connie Angel smiled in a shy, new way she had and let him fix Nellie's nosebag. After that, Bert Angel handed Sprog a large brass candlestick.

"What do you think of that?"

"Very nice," said Sprog.

"Nice?" sniffed Bert Angel. "That won't bring home the groceries. How much do you think it's worth?"

Sprog thought. "Twenty-five pence?"

Bert Angel did a quick translation and said, disgustedly, "Five bob! Go on, *feel* it."

Sprog said, "I *am* feeling it."

"I mean, weigh it in your hands."

When Sprog had jigged it up and down a rapacious

gleam appeared in Bert Angel's eyes.

"Heavy, isn't it? You know why? Because it's solid — solid brass. I wouldn't part with a pair of them for less than a fiver." He winked. "I'm not saying that if I was pushed I wouldn't take four — I'm not what you'd call a greedy man, myself. On the other hand you've got to live." He took the candlestick out of Sprog's hands, carefully, as if it was made of glass, not brass.

Then he put a boiled sweet in his mouth and gave Sprog a lesson: "You get called into a house, on account of somebody having a pair of candlesticks to sell. You don't rush in all eager, like. You act *blasé*, got it? *Blasé*. You're doing the party a favour, going into their house and looking at candlesticks. You act polite, mind, but you keep a look on your face that says the last thing you want to see is a candlestick. You've been collecting candlesticks all morning, before breakfast, and you're sick of the sight of 'em. After a bit of humming and hawing, you make an offer — ten bob, say. If the party's got any sense, they'll push you up a bit. That's all right because it makes them feel better to think they're putting a fast one over on you. So after a while you up the price a bit — say to a quid. That makes them see what a decent bloke you are — the sort who goes round giving away free pound notes. Got it?"

"Got it," said Sprog.

"Well, let's go home for breakfast."

It was Sprog's first invitation to Number Twenty-nine Beak Street. At first look, the Angels' home might have been a branch of the business; strips of unmatching carpet, cracked vases on the mantlepiece, a rusty bird cage, containing a canary, by the window; a cracked clock on the wall and a dresser full of standing plates and swinging cups — all left-overs from different sets. On a rickety bamboo table stood an old square TV and a hefty china chamber pot with painted roses and real, prickly cactus plants.

A cosy fire burned in the grate and Sprog felt its warmth penetrate his skin. A different, deeper glow enveloped him, too: here was a door he need not listen at, a window where he could show his face.

Without his cap, Bert Angel's head was bald and bony and his ears stuck out. He gave the fire a poke with his toes.

"We're taking some stuff up the market this morning. You can come along, if you fancy. Anything to eat, Connie?" He gave Sprog one of his drily humorous, solemn glances. "To look inside our pantry lately, you'd think an army of ants had been clean through it."

Connie pretended not to hear. She tweeted at the canary and gave it bird seed. Then she crossed to a corner shelf occupied by a box with a wire front.

"What have you got in there?" asked Sprog.

"A mouse," said Connie Angel.

Bert Angel sounded wryly exasperated. "A *house* mouse! Connie caught it in the pantry, eating porridge oats. She's been keeping it in that box ever since. Connie could tame a dragon without even singeing her eyebrows. Personally, I'd have busted its back with a poker and been done with it. I'm not a great animal lover, myself — unless they earn their keep."

In the scullery Connie left some bacon frying and some toast on the grill. Without letting anything get burnt, she filled up the bits of waiting time by attending to the inhabitants of a much bigger hutch standing on the floor beside an old fashioned copper.

Connie knelt beside the hutch, tweeting lovingly, letting at least three guinea pigs in turn nibble her fingers through the wire. Her eyes were warm and quickened. Sprog sauntered out to take an interest.

"Nice, aren't they?" he said.

Connie said, "The hutch is too small, really."

From the living room Bert Angel grunted, "*All* hutches are too small. Can't see much point in shutting things up, myself."

Connie had opened the hutch door and taken one of the guinea pigs in her hands. She held it a little too tight, a little too earnestly.

"To keep them safe," she said, very softly.

It was early dusk when Sprog got back. The arch door was locked so he tapped the secret signal — once, twice, three times . . . There was a faint snuffle behind the door, followed by the dog's whine. Then silence.

Sprog had the uncanny feeling that the Boy was awake and listening — listening and deliberately not answering. He was letting the thick, opaque door separate him from Sprog. The *new* Sprog? The Sprog who dressed in dandy clothes and spent his day with people called the Angels; who came back with flushed face to count out his earnings and brag about his exploits in a different world?

Sprog began kicking at the door, partly out of pique, partly in case the Boy was, after all, merely over-sleeping. But eventually the door swung back — grudgingly and squeakingly as if blown in by a draught.

The arch was in darkness and somewhere was the Boy — but Sprog located him only by the fretful presence of his mutt. Sprog pulled the door closed and turned the key.

"What's got into you, mate?" He groped for Connie's battery lamp. As he switched it on the draught blew in again and the shadow of the Boy stood briefly against the evening sky.

"It isn't properly dark, yet," said Sprog, but the door slammed.

The arch was a shambles; it was as if the Boy were still present in the scatter of his belongings. Bits of his restless day lay left behind: a jagged empty food tin, a half eaten bun, the clothes Connie had brought for him, but which he never wore, strewn over the floor. Even Sprog's own shelf had not escaped; the blankets were tangled, the remains of an egg lay smashed at the foot and, sitting on the pillow as significant and insulting as a rude gesture of fingers, was the faded, much weathered woollen cap. The old Sprog had given him that.

"Ruddy marvellous, i'nit?" said Sprog, aloud. "He's mucked up *my* bed an' all."

Then he saw the golliwog. The Boy must have climbed up the shelves and fetched it down, for it sprawled inelegantly against a wooden support where the Boy's feet would reach; where, as he lay in bed consumed with his own thoughts, he would be face to face with it — across a distance. The golliwog smirked at Sprog in the lamplight and he kicked it off the bed in a burst of petulance — angry at what he could feel but did not understand.

Outside on the waste ground, where the kids played in the graveyard of chassis, where there were rumours of foxes, a lame dog, not unlike a fox in the falling darkness, zig-zagged in and out of the junk heaps making for the dip. It moved awkwardly, but fast, and the underside of its tail was a white flash across the tangled green.

At the edge of the dip it stood off its guard, obsessed with the scent it found there — and the nearest of the kids, lingering in the twilight to end their game, saw it at once. They were too wise to shout, though foolish enough to believe that a real fox would stand there, in three-legged complacency, awaiting capture — or was it not a belief but a *wish*?

A boy in a cowboy suit — hat, gun holsters and lasso — approached the creature from behind, loop of rope ready, encouraged by less equipped, less bold kids bent behind the car bodies. A flip, and the noose was tightening about the mongrel's neck — then the shout went up: "We've got the fox, we've got the fox!"

The boy in the cowboy suit clung tight, perhaps wondering, for the first time, what you did with a fox when you caught it — especially a fox which was so lacking in ferocious response, so meek and cur-like, that it scarcely seemed worth catching at all.

Suddenly a new and strange figure half appeared on the scene. At first, no one glimpsed its face, seeing only a shadow with sticks for legs and a turnip head. Then, as it drew nearer, its loping gait marked it as something more grotesque than a human child. In the days to come, how differently the tales were told: a giant, it was said, or a pygmy. It was real, or a ghost. Yet all the stories told of something horrific and scarcely to be whispered about the face. A face without shape, they said; a face like a mask made the more hideous by pin prick eyes — a face to be run from.

But meanwhile the boy with the lasso scrambled

away from the dip, leaving fox, rope and hat behind, and darted for the wreck where the others crouched. At first, curiosity and a call in the blood kept them from flight. Here was something *else* out of the wild; something they might hunt down, root out from any retreat it made for. Together, and at a safe distance they searched the growing darkness for a witch to hunt or a bear to bait.

But there was now no breath of sound from the dip. Huddled in a tight, frightened, expectant knot they crept out of hiding and there was nothing there; no fox, no monster — only wisps of a nightmare memory. *Something* had come and gone, but all that lay in the long grass was a piece of twisted rope.

The winter nights passed and the days brought to light strange happenings. Stories were spun like sagas. Thefts . . . small, bright things removed from upstairs rooms in sleeping houses. There were harsher tales of wilful damage; slashed furniture, potted plants upturned, pantries raided. Sleepers wakened by weird sounds: "like an animal," they said. A chicken house left open, the hens found next morning rooting in a cabbage bed. A ruffled parrot, a frightened cat, a swinging gate . . . a shed door wrenched from its hinges.

It? A predator of slim build and extraordinarily agile frame; a shadow on a waste pipe near an upper window. Could anything bigger than a sparrow fly through a fanlight in a third-floor flat? Did *It* leave those muddy footprints in the porch, and what sent a loose tile scudding down a roof. *It?*

Chapter Thirteen

On Fridays, when he needed to be early on the spot to help Bert Angel with his round next morning, Sprog spent the night at the house in Beak Street, sleeping on a mattress under the stairs. It was cosy and homely and muffled-quiet, with an electric meter ticking like a friendly cockroach.

He would awaken to the smell of bacon and eggs and find Connie Angel bent over the scullery stove, hair wispy, eyes turned thoughtfully for a moment on Sprog. He knew she would slip out, presently, to take breakfast along for the Boy and his dog — after she had fed the canary by the window, the house mouse on the shelf and the guinea pigs in the scullery.

Bert Angel took Sprog's comings and goings for granted. "If there's anything special you fancy, you just let on," he said, once.

"Like what?" said Sprog.

"Well, like a bath for instance. We've only got a tin one, hanging on a nail in the scullery, but we can soon heat you some water."

"Do I pong?" asked Sprog.

"That's not what I meant," said Bert Angel.

Sprog said, "I don't have to bother you. When I want a bath I go up the swimming pool."

"Good swimmer are you?" said Bert Angel.

"Not really," said Sprog. "But you get just as clean

whether you can swim or not." Sprog felt embarrassed because he couldn't remember the last time he had been to a pool. On the other hand, he had got caught in the rain a few times and that was better than nothing.

Sprog's absences from the arch were longer and more frequent. Other images filled his mind when he was walking along a street or riding the junk cart: the dance of yellow flames in the fire that Bert Angel would keep stoked with the toe of his shoe, the pale light under the dusty lamp shade, the Angels themselves . . . their silences, their little bursts of talk, their slow smiles, the smell and touch of their skin and breath. Sprog wanted the Boy to share this sort of home, yet, guiltily, he wanted it all for himself; he wanted to be with the Boy, but he mostly wanted to be with the Angels.

Connie sometimes told Sprog the stories she had heard, but only when they were alone. Bert Angel wasn't letting on. A wink, a wry smile, a sniff, a suck of a fruit gum — that was Bert's way with rumours. Or: "I don't take no notice of a lot of gossip. I'm a man who keeps himself to himself, myself."

Sprog still slept most nights in the dollmaker's workshop. Late one afternoon, when he'd finished helping Bert deliver some furniture to an auction, he said cheerio, let himself out the back way as usual, pushed through the broken gate, turned under the railway bridge and along the arch faces. The cold bit, the darkness was extra dark. The lights shining along the railway had haloes of frozen mist.

The Boy hadn't gone out yet and in the arch you could have hacked the air with an ice pick. The Boy had let the stove out — he often did. He was awake, leaning against his shelf post, watching Sprog tip the paraffin

111

can. He had the golliwog between his knees and was making it jig up and down, its floppy, grinning head tearing stitches. The dog lay on its sack, shivering forlornly, one eye on Sprog, tail tapping the floor.

When Sprog turned from the stove the Boy was dressing. The mutt sprang up in anticipation.

"Do you have to go out?" asked Sprog. The Boy gave Sprog one of his unfathomable looks. "I mean, it's cold and there's a fog coming up. Why not stop in for once?"

The draught from the door seemed to suck Boy and dog into their night.

Sprog got his supper — Connie Angel had been in some time that day with a dish of cold sausages. The arch roof loomed gloomier every minute — perhaps the battery in the lamp was giving out. Sprog thought of slipping back to the Angels', but what was wrong with stopping on his own? Sprog had always got by on his own, even before he had tagged on to the Boy. He was okay on his own.

He spent a long time counting his wages. By now there was a lot of silver and copper and even a few pound notes in a tobacco tin which he kept at the bottom of his old duffle bag. He hadn't spent any of it yet — anyone would think he was saving up. For what? He hadn't nicked anything for weeks, either.

Sprog thought, I'm different. I *feel* different. Why don't I go out and live it up? Why stop in this dump, getting the bleeding miseries?

But at the thought of wind in the streets, streets over-familiar, now, and offering no new lure of adventure, Sprog nestled under his blanket instead and dozed. He woke and dozed again. Once he thought he heard the cockroach tick of the meter under the Angels' stairs, but it was the stove guttering out.

It was some time in the middle of the night when the door burst open. The sudden draught, the click of a latch, then quick breathing, panting, sobbing.

Sprog reached for his torch. The Boy flinched in the beam and tried to find new shadows, moving in quick, jerky strides like a clockwork doll with its works jammed.

Sprog followed the Boy with his torch, eventually pinning him on his shelf bed.

The Boy had his hands to his face, and blood trickled through his fingers. Sprog went to him and wrenched the hands away. There was an ugly gash in the furrowed skin of his forehead. "Nasty," said Sprog. "What did you do, mate? Come clean through a barbed wire fence?"

He fetched water from the closet and made the Boy lie down so that he could clean the cut. It wasn't all that bad once the clotting blood was wiped away: it was terror, more than pain, which still lurked in the Boy's eyes.

Sprog got the Boy to bed, then he went and locked the door. The mutt followed him there and back, its frightened eyes a duplicate of the Boy's.

"What happened out there?" Sprog asked the mongrel. "You get caught on the nick? Trouble, was it? Well, you've been asking for it, from what they say."

It wagged its tail as though Sprog had been praising it. The mutt wanted to talk — it was like a human trying to get out.

The Boy's eyes opened again. Sprog said, "Things are hotting up, aren't they, mate? Want to scarper off, find some other place? And d'you still want me along an' all?"

An answer lay in the Boy's steady look back. He had taken his eyes out of his dark, secretive world and given them back to Sprog – the *old* Sprog.

And the old Sprog said with his old, intimate cockiness, "Well, it's easy. I told you about the panic kit in the shed, didn't I? All we got to do is grab it and run. Soon as you like. Tomorrow?" It was suddenly what Sprog wanted. The *real* Sprog?

The Boy closed his eyes and slept.

Sprog slept. He awoke before first light brightened the oval glass, got up and relit the stove.

While he was waiting for Connie Angel he sat at the bench by the dimming lamp, keeping the rays from the Boy's sleeping face, flicking through some old magazines Connie had once brought.

He came across some pictures of the seaside. The pictures showed a crowded beach with yellow sand and a wide, blue sea beyond. There was a pier and deck chairs and, in the distance, a domed funfair with roundabouts and a big dipper and stalls.

Connie Angel tapped on the door. Sprog unlocked it and she came in. The Boy sat up, staring at the door, and the mutt limped over and brushed its head against her leg.

Connie started to unpack the carrier. Sprog said, "You needn't have bothered with that lot." Her hands paused on the tins. "We're off, me and the Boy."

Connie Angel stood very still. She was looking over Sprog's shoulder at the seaside picture.

Sprog shrugged. "I just had this idea, see? It may sound daft, but . . . well, it won't be winter for ever. Me

114

and the Boy thought we might hop it down to the sea. We'd be all right there, wouldn't we? You know what I'd do? I'd try and get a job running a stall. A shooting gallery, say, or flogging icecream or candy floss. You don't have to laugh."

Connie Angel wasn't laughing. Her eyes switched to the Boy. Sprog went on, "Look at his head! He got a bashing last night. Somebody scared hell out of him, an' all. I never seen him so scared. Well, I don't reckon he's done half the things they say, but I've got to get him out before they get their mitts on him — haven't I?"

Connie went to the Boy who had lain back when he'd seen it was Connie. She leant over him, stroking his head with her thin, gentle fingers. The blood had dried, but there was purple swelling under the skin. He did not flinch away and after a moment his eyes glazed and closed. Connie took the golliwog from the end of his shelf and tucked it under the blanket with its twisted head on the Boy's shoulder. Then she came back to the bench.

Sprog wriggled on the stool. "You can have all me clothes back and that. Ta for everything. Say thanks to your dad, an' all. He's a decent old codger."

Connie Angel seemed very tall. She said, in a whisper, "No, tell him yourself!"

Then she turned her back, opened the door, pushed the mutt gently back in and shut the door again.

Sprog was glad that bit was over. Now he'd wait for the Boy to wake up and they'd get through the day, somehow, until it was dark again.

The Boy slept on. Every time Sprog moved the dog got under his feet, thinking they were going somewhere. When he kicked its rump, more or less accidentally, it stood by the door, whining softly.

"Shuddup!" said Sprog. "You sound like Connie Angel's canary."

Still the Boy slept.

Sprog changed into his old jeans and torn anorak. He collected all his new clothes together and pushed them into a big empty bag. Then he put the bag on his shoulder, glanced at the Boy, prodded the mutt away from the arch door, and set out for Bert Angel's shop.

Bert Angel was alone, except for Nellie the horse. He was seated at his little desk deep inside the arch, screwing his eyes up under the electric light bulb. He didn't seem surprised to see Sprog; neither, apparently, did he notice the bag which Sprog dropped on the floor.

"I hear you're off to the seaside," said Bert Angel

"Go on?" said Sprog. "Well, maybe."

"Not a great one for the seaside, myself," said the junk man. "Can't say I care for the country all that much, either. Give me a great big town full of smoke any time. Sort of feel at home in the town. I always thought you felt the same."

"The seaside is a sort of town."

"Sort of," agreed Bert Angel, "but you can't get about far, can you? Not with all that sea in the way. Claustrophobic, that's what I think of the seaside, myself."

Bert Angel handed over his sweets and put one in his own mouth. "What makes you fancy the seaside?"

"I dunno," said Sprog. "It's nice and warm, by the sea."

"Not always it ain't," said Bert Angel. "And even when it is hot, it stinks of seaweed. There's no regular trade at the seaside, neither. Take icecreams. How many

116

days in an English summer do you reckon you can make a profit selling icecreams? Me and Connie popped down to Margate one day last year. Rained cats and dogs. Never saw the sun again till we was coming back through Deptford."

"It was just a thought," said Sprog.

Bert Angel put the pencil in his ear, waved Sprog to a chair and said, his eyes suddenly sharp, "I've been doing some thinking, too. I hear we've got problems."

"We have?" said Sprog.

Bert Angel looked at Sprog for a long time and when he went on talking it was different from usual; as if he had worked out in advance just what he was going to say. "We've never asked you questions, me and Connie. That's not to say we haven't done some wondering. Where you come from, for instance, and how you got here."

"By train," said Sprog. "Sort of. Before that . . ."

"Go on," said Bert Angel.

Sprog told him — about being found on a church doorstep when he was a titch, then the Home, and fostering, and running away, and pilfering — the lot. He didn't hold anything back; he wasn't going to tell lies to Bert Angel.

Bert Angel shifted the sweet to the other side of his mouth and said, "Well, me and Connie have got a kind of deal in mind. We'd have to work a few things out, though. I mean, we can't shut our eyes to facts. There's the Law, for instance and I'm a law-abiding man, myself. So far we haven't had nosey parkers calling but sooner or later somebody's going to ask awkward questions, like how come I'm letting you tag on with me in the junk business, off and on, when you ought to be at school."

"Come again?" said Sprog. In his short, varied life Sprog had given thought to many things. School, however, had never been one of them.

"You don't have to look as if you'd just been hit by a ten pound hammer. You've got to go to school, sooner or later. Connie goes to school and she don't complain. It'd be better to do it voluntary than be dragged there by your ear. You could still help out with the business on Saturdays and holidays. Some day we might be partners, you and me, and you can't run a business unless you're good at figuring and reading up catalogues and knowing what's what. Personally, I'm all for a bit of education, myself."

"Hey, hold on!" said Sprog. Bert Angel was telling him so many different things that Sprog couldn't be sure which was the most important. "You're going too fast for me."

"What I'm saying," went on Bert Angel, "is that we could do things for you, me and Connie — like offering you a home, for keeps. We'd have to square things with the busy bodies, but from what Connie tells me you don't really belong anywhere, so you might as well belong with us." Bert Angel held the sweet bag out again. "How does it sound to you?"

"I don't know," said Sprog. "Ta! Only . . . I wouldn't know how to tell . . . the Boy."

"Can't do much for him," said Bert Angel. "I only wish we could. Not that it's any use telling Connie that — she seems to think it would be as easy as taking on an extra guinea pig."

"He wouldn't want that," said Sprog.

"No," said Bert Angel. "That's what I told Connie.

Maybe we'll think of some other way of helping him. As for you — well, turn it over in your mind. If you come in with us it'll have to be because *you* want it, not because we say so." Bert Angel sat back reflectively. "I'm not what you'd call a philosophical man, but as I see it, the Almighty slapped a great belt of fresh air round this planet, with more than enough for everybody to breathe. For those who can fly in it, that's their privilege, but we haven't all got wings. On the other hand, we have all got noses and if everybody sniffs their own fresh air that's all right by me. Personally, I don't see why anybody should go about clipping clothes pegs to other people's noses — myself."

The fog lingered along the river. All that day Sprog hid by the river, hid in the fog. It got into his old, thin clothes; it seeped into his eyes and ears, it twirled and fuzzed and froze in his very thoughts.

He stole nothing, ate nothing, decided nothing.

When he came back along the arch faces, fog was thickening over the waste ground. A low, red sun made pink shadows and out of the shadows, out of the fog, came the voices of children at play on the abandoned car bodies.

Sprog's hand hesitated on the knob of the arch door, then he pushed it open. They were awake, they were waiting. The Boy, with anorak and woollen cap, rucksack packed by his feet; the mutt looking up expectantly with a twitch of its tail; the golliwog, sitting up against the rucksack, legs splayed . . . was he coming, too?

They were all waiting for Sprog and Sprog didn't know what to say.

There they sat: the Boy, his dog and the golliwog, as if they were waiting for a train and they thought Sprog had a ticket, too.

And then, as Sprog tried to tell the truth there came three taps — Connie Angel's code, Connie's taps . . . Sprog let her in. She looked at the Boy waiting with his luggage. Then her eyes turned on Sprog. She thought he was going after all, so Sprog had to say it. He *had* to.

"I'm not coming, mate. Sorry, but I'm not coming. You can go, soon as it's dark. You know where the panic kit is. Yours is the green bag. I'm stopping behind, see?

Chapter Fourteen

The Boy's eyes were terrible in their uncomprehending. As he picked up his rucksack, Connie Angel stood between him and the door. She was never afraid of his face. She seemed to see, without effort, behind the scars into the strangeness, the sickness, the long hurt. "Don't go . . . out there." She whispered, as though soft words alone might make him stay.

The Boy watched Connie's lips then his gaze moved to Sprog. He pushed past, his dog hobbling beside him. He seemed to have forgotten the golliwog. He reached the door and turned the knob. Then with one brief look back he heaved the rucksack to his shoulder and, leaving the door open, loped across the railway path, vanishing down the embankment.

"I'm going to make sure he gets clear," said Sprog. "Coming?"

As they scrambled down the bank the fog temporarily lifted, writhing away in great, grey shifting clouds. The chassis, the fences and buildings beyond, the playing kids — everything was starkly outlined in the sinking sun's red rays. Connie looked anxiously at Sprog then her eyes sought the Boy. She was thinking of what would become of her canary if it should fly through the window: a short, glad freedom, a burst of song . . . then the tearing of wings, the scatter of feathers, the fall from the sky. And what would happen to a white sparrow in search of a nest?

The dog made straight for the dip and the Boy went after it towards the hidden shed. The kids saw them both: the electric news crackled over the waste ground: The fox has come back. Then: *It* is here!

The Boy sensed the danger and crouched low as if he thought the grass could hide him. But there was no darkness to hide his face and the kids had him in a bright, red desert as transparent as an uncurtained window.

rom all quarters they began slowly closing in, filtering in small groups between the car bodies. They helped themselves to weapons from rubbish heaps; sticks, bars, stones. As they crept in a huge perimeter towards the dip they beat on rusty tins with sticks, shouting in shrill voices like Indian beaters flushing out a tiger.

The Boy crouched deep in the dip, clutching at grass, the dog keeping close beside him. Then, quite suddenly, the red sunset died behind the tall buildings and Boy and dog were received into darkness.

Losing sight of them, Connie Angel and Sprog mingled with the kids nearest the dip. The shouting and drum beating stopped, somebody picked up a trail and, in the deepening darkness, torches began to flash, sweeping the fence and the road behind it.

The kids poured through a gap in the fence, keeping tight hold of sticks. There was a running scuffle of feet on a road by a tall building giving back echoes. They twisted in and out of streets and alleys, getting nearer the river, deeper into another haze of fog.

The dog came back, limping unnoticed through legs, seeking out Connie and Sprog. For it to have lost the

Boy he must have run fast — too fast for a crippled dog. Connie Angel patted it then they ran on behind the scurrying feet ahead.

They reached a high wharfside with an endless row of tall, spikey railings, shutting off any way down. Here and there were locked iron gates above long flights of stone steps vanishing into the fog.

Someone must have seen the Boy, or his shadow, approach a certain point in the fence. One group of kids was working its way along the railings, while another, with Sprog, Connie and dog hanging back, formed the second half of a pincer movement closing in to meet it. The fugitive must have got through, or over, somewhere. Yet the seven foot railings had tips as sharp as spears and there was a double strand of twisted barbed wire along the top.

It was a long time before anyone found the right spot. There was a short conference, then one of the kids took off his jacket and, reaching up on his toes, flung it over the top of a wired gate above a set of steps. Another gave him a leg up and the kid scrambled over, tearing his clothes but making a safe landing. A second kid got over, then a third. They went off, light footed, down the steps towards the sound of water washing against a wall.

The dog bristled, whined and hobbled to and fro behind the railings. It tried to squeeze through, but the bars were set too close together. Sprog wanted to go over with the advance party, but Connie was shivering and miserable and he stayed with her.

Had the Boy got down to the river? The kids seemed sure of it, but in Sprog's opinion if he'd had any sense he would have doubled back and lost himself in the foggy streets. He knew the Boy a lot better than they did.

Sprog went back, looking for a gap which the Boy might have used. Then he found it! It was in one of the gates at the top of a set of steps — the kids must have missed it. Two of the bars had been bent back in a double arc making enough room to wriggle through. When the Boy was trapped and scared, what were metal bars to him? Sprog got through and waited for Connie.

Footsteps came along the street and torches swished. The kids saw the gap and half a dozen poured through after Sprog and Connie. They clattered in an eager bunch down the foggy steps.

Sprog got down first. There was a narrow ledge of quayside with rusty chains and bollards — but no boats. The dark river water lapped oily and close at Sprog's feet. From the quay there was no way along in either direction. There was only a sheer river wall, slippery to the touch, and a narrow quay jutting out into the river.

One of the kids shone a torch. The rest stood with sticks limp in their hands. The dog stood at the edge of the quay barking frantically at the water. Then it hobbled back to Connie and Sprog and whined again. The kids could hardly see the mutt, but they heard it, turned round and looked at Connie, then at Sprog. Connie they knew, but they didn't know Sprog. Sprog found himself his own bit of darkness, not wanting their curiosity.

They all stayed down on the quay, lingering, looking out at the speckled water, watching the hazy passage of river traffic. The lights from buildings made misty pillars of golden light in the water. On the surface were patches of white which might have been flotsam — or a swimmer. But the Boy could not have swum for so long as this. The dark, dappled, oily water with its soft, sinister waves gave back only one answer . . . and the dog, whining at the quay's edge, was keeping a mournful wake.

"You've as good as drowned him," said Sprog, out of his darkness, out of his anonymity. "If you'd chucked him in, you couldn't have made more bleeding sure of it."

The faces tried to materialize Sprog out of his darkness, but nobody spoke. A couple of kids threw their sticks far out into the river.

Downstream came a new brightness out of the thinning fog. The moon was rising out of the water, a great half ball, an unreal yellow light, haloed at its edge. It lay on the black water like a huge, silver arch, the mouth of a tunnel filled with white fire. It was sucking in the black water and everything, dead and alive, on its surface and in its depths.

Sprog realized that the dog had vanished. Nobody but he seemed to have noticed − until Sprog saw that Connie Angel was looking, puzzled, up the steps. The dog may have crept, defeated, up the long, stone staircase, but that was not the way of the dog. They remembered no splash, had observed no speck of phosphorescence marking its course into the river. A little while ago it had crouched whimpering at the edge of the quay; now it was gone.

The kids drifted away up the steps, and soon Sprog and Connie Angel were alone together on the quay. The moon rose higher over the river. The fog had rolled away after all, and stars twinkled bright and new born. The river throbbed and swelled, a great life-giving artery so that it became harder to think of death — the death of a Boy, or even the death of a dog.

Connie Angel took Sprog's arm as they left the river quay. Half way up the steps she was shocked to hear Sprog laughing quietly in the darkness.

"What's funny?"

"I reckon I've got it," said Sprog. "He never was daft, you know, the Boy. He had to run for it sometimes same as me. But . . . well, he always ran *somewhere*, see? I reckon he had it all thought out. You never knew the Boy like I did. You know what I think? He nicked a boat. I bet all the time we was crying our eyes out he was sitting in a boat, having us all on. He even kidded his mutt, at first — and then I bet he whistled it."

"I didn't hear a whistle," said Connie Angel.

"Sometimes it was sort of high pitched. You couldn't hear it if you was human, only see his lips move, but the mutt could."

Through the gap in the railings, Connie Angel shivered and wrapped herself about with her arms. "If you're wrong, the dog will come back," she said.

"Don't be too hopeful!" said Sprog. "It won't come back. They're out there, somewhere, laughing. Only the Boy never laughed . . . I'm going to miss him, you know. The Boy, I mean — and his mutt. It was a nice mutt."

Connie Angel said, "If you think he stole a boat and is out there somewhere, shouldn't we let on to the police?"

"Oh, give over," said Sprog. "He'd rather be drowned, would the Boy, than be nicked by a copper."

The end of the story? No, for it is not that easy to catch

a sparrow! Sometimes, when he was with the Angels, Sprog had the feeling that the Boy was sitting on his shoulder, doll-sized. Yet, when he tried to picture the Boy — where he was, what he was doing, how he was feeling, Sprog could see only a wide river flowing into a silver tunnel. Then the Angel's house in Beak Street felt too small, the walls a little too close, the ceilings a bit too low. Such traitorous, ungrateful thoughts Sprog kept to himself.

Sprog and Connie went along to tidy up the arch. There wasn't much to do. They wrapped up blankets, put dolls straight on the shelves and swept the floor. What was left behind — the oil stove, the cooker, the cutlery and crockery — they carried to the junk shop and put back in stock. Sprog had a bad moment when he picked up the enamel bowl the mutt had eaten from and another when he climbed up the shelves to replace the grinning golliwog near the curved ceiling. Apart from the golliwog the Boy had left nothing behind — not even a keepsake.

Sprog nearly said to Connie Angel, "I've just remembered, I've got me panic kit over in that shed. We ought to go and fetch it."

But he didn't. The panic kit sat, not only in the shed at the top of the dip, but in a small corner of Sprog's mind, which still had, as it were, a back door.

When he was out in the light again, Sprog cheered up. A last glimpse into the arch showed a dark emptiness; but darkness was only a curtain you hid behind when there was a reason to hide. Sprog, after all, was different from the Boy. The Boy had wanted to escape into darkness whereas Sprog's yearning was for the light — and what was lighter than life with the Angels?

127

Only, sometimes, the light seemed to shine through bars — and what was the difference if they were made of solid gold?

One night Sprog lay on his mattress under the Angels' stairs and the ticking of the electric meter suddenly sounded like a time bomb. He got up, switched on his torch and packed his duffle bag.

Taking nothing belonging to the Angels, only some of the clothes he had been given, he let himself out through the back door, pushing it very softly behind him. Then he walked in moonlight under the railway bridge, on beside the arches, down the dewy embankment and across to the shed at the edge of the dip.

He worked on the screws. The panic kit was still there under the floor boards; the Boy's too — he had never collected it. Sprog dragged his own out and heaved it to his shoulder. Then he found the gap in the fence and hit the road.

The street was wide and long and free, the star-lit sky the highest ceiling in the world.

Now and then Sprog looked over his shoulder, having a weird suspicion that Connie Angel was following, but the pavement resounded only with his runaway footsteps.

Chapter Fifteen

Sprog stowed away on a fruit and vegetable lorry heading — it was a fair guess — for Covent Garden Market.

On the journey, when he wasn't eating oranges, apples and bananas, he packed as much of the panic kit as possible into his familiar duffle bag. Some of the spare clothes wouldn't squeeze in so he wore them in layers — two vests, three shirts and an extra pullover — under his anorak. He emptied his tobacco tin money box and buttoned the notes into a pocket, keeping the coins handy in his jeans.

Central London was unexplored territory for Sprog, an over-populated planet encircled by dazzling, coloured suns and throbbing with volcanic sound.

Of uncertain age, plump on account of the extra clothing he carried, Sprog managed, by one ruse or another, to create the impression that he was never quite alone and unsupervised. He was particularly careful not to look too lost. The renowned kindness of policemen to small, lost boys was notorious.

Whenever he could, he tagged on to one of the many school parties which were disgorged from coaches or shepherded in long queues out of Charing Cross station. In a spell of bright, sharp, winter sunshine he helped feed pigeons in Trafalgar Square. He tagged on to a bunch of country kids up to see the sights; eight or nine,

Sprog reckoned they were. Sprog could be eight or nine whenever he fancied; eyes big, mouth quirky, his older brain sizing up chances.

Sprog got talking to a kid who might have been his twin brother for he had straw-coloured hair, a freckly nose and even carried an old duffle bag, only with a different football team printed on the side.

"They're no good," said the kid, meaning the team on Sprog's duffle bag. "Next to bottom in the league."

"At least they're not dirty like your lot," said Sprog, with friendly rivalry.

The other boy took a packet of sandwiches out of his duffle bag. He fed pigeons and every feathered ruffian in London seemed to home on him, perching on his arms and head and shoulders till he looked like a bird man.

"Here you are," said the kid. "You feed them." He gave Sprog a sandwich and Sprog fed himself. To hell with the pigeons!

In the course of a couple of days Sprog got free trips to Madame Tussauds', the Planetarium, St Paul's Cathedral and two different museums. He nearly got on a visit to the Zoo, but there wasn't room in the coach. Teachers in charge of school parties had a way of counting heads and that could be awkward. On the other hand as Sprog soon learned, they rarely worried if there was one head too many, only if there was one too few.

When he couldn't find a school party, Sprog lost himself in crowds of window shoppers. He blued most of his savings that way. He bought himself a canary--coloured shirt he fancied and a jazzy tie to go with it. He spent three pounds on a smart wristwatch and another on a fine pocket knife with two switch blades, a corkscrew and a bit for cleaning nails. Next to the knife was a display of key rings. One of them had a tiny golliwog attached to a chain and Sprog thought, for a moment, how much the Boy would fancy it. Then he realized that the Boy had gone, but Sprog bought it as a keepsake.

He bought himself a real sit-down meal; eggs and chips and apple pie and ice cream and coffee to finish with. He blued quite a lot on a best seat at the pictures and he took several long roundabout rides on the underground. The nights were more difficult than the days. No darkness fell on the city. The lights burned on and only gradually did the crowd diminish and the traffic grow more sparse. Policemen began to appear at alarmingly frequent intervals and Sprog had to duck.

Sprog had never fancied public toilets as places to sleep in; besides, they were about as safe as baited mouse traps. Station waiting rooms were not much better. They were okay for a quick stopover, a toast by a radiator or boiler, but hanging about in them could be disastrous. Porters and cleaners arrived, carrying brooms like weapons; and outside policemen waited in pairs, one to do the shouting, the other to do the nabbing. And if you fell asleep in the pictures, you were all too likely to be swept up with the sweet papers and cigarette ends.

In Sprog's experience, this city was never more overcrowded than at night. When all the people he had rubbed up against during the day had gone to bed, a new race took over; a strangely sub-human night shift with pale faces and tangled hair and sad, suspicious mouths and muted voices; and bulky clothes made up of spare jersies — a race of guardians and busybodies armed with brushes and brooms and flashlights.

Their slow night tread took the measure of every damp, dark street and alley. They had owl's eyes with which to probe into every shadow, bat's ears attuned to the slightest discordant sound and they often seemed dedicated to hunting the Sprogs of this world. Hearts heavy with the night hours lightened at the very thought of tracking him down; and on more than one occasion, Sprog nearly found himself pinned like a specimen in a patch of torchlight, ringed about by these night people who would ask questions, dither among themselves, make anxious enquiries as to the wisdom of digging some sleeping Authority out of bed.

All through his first day Sprog half promised himself a night in a swank hotel; but very late, when he had come out of the pictures, Sprog knew that he had used up too much of his money. In any case, the idea seemed far more daunting now that it had come to the point. From bits of TV, Sprog had assembled a composite picture of commissionaires rocking on their heels, shifty-eyed bellhops making furtive telephone calls, and of chandeliers spilling light on broad staircases.

Not that Sprog entirely abandoned the possibility of a hotel. He came out of the cinema past the statue of Eros in Piccadilly Circus and went along Shaftesbury Avenue, keeping close to the walls and shop fronts. A bitter wind was blowing down the street, cutting like knives through his several layers of clothing, and Sprog wanted his bed.

He left the broad-lit thoroughfare as soon as he could and vanished into the shadows of a cobbled alley threading its way along the back of the buildings. There, when the dazzle had gone out of his eyes, he searched doorways and steps and yards for a likely haven. Eventually his nostrils picked up the smell of food and Sprog instinctively homed on it.

He went through a narrow yard full of packing cases and boxes and then up a set of railinged steps on to a flat, concrete area at the top. There were more packing cases there — big ones — and from the wall on his left, out of a close-meshed iron grating, came a low, gentle growl. As soon as Sprog crept past it, he could feel warm air wafting towards him, as from an open oven.

Sprog carefully dragged one of the wooden packing cases nearer the big vent, turning it so that the open side faced the grille. Then he crawled into the packing case and, as of old, wrapped himself in the blanket and used his now well-stuffed duffle bag as a pillow.

The night was uneventful and Sprog woke in good time. It was not yet light, but from somewhere behind the warm grille came the tantalizing smell of frying bacon and the rattle of crockery. When Sprog packed his things and crawled cautiously out of the box, he noticed that there was a door beside the grille. Sprog wasn't trying anything clever, though. He still had enough of Bert Angel's wages to buy himself breakfast.

He made his stealthy way back to the cobbled alley, then looked back, getting his bearings. High up on the roof, immediately over where he had slept, he had a sideways view of a neon sign in big, blood red letters: EROS HOTEL. He heaved the duffle bag on his shoulder and stepped out for the main street. The pavement was already crowded and Sprog saw no need for subterfuge. He walked the stiffness out of his joints and went down the Haymarket in search of a cafe. He'd have no trouble finding his hotel again.

That evening Sprog kept himself warm in an amusement arcade, blued some more of his savings on the machines, then went back to his hotel. The second night was much like the first, except that Sprog didn't sleep so well. He dreamed about Connie Angel and the Boy; and Bert Angel was giving him sweets, then removing his cap and scratching his bald head. Once, when Sprog awoke in the pitch darkness, his dreams lingered on for some time and he knew he was waiting for three soft taps on the arch door. When he crawled out of his box to meet the new day, he found that a sprinkle of new, fine snow had settled on the yard steps.

That day — the third — Sprog spent almost the last of his money on a slap-up meal. It was breakfast, so he didn't get dinner, tea or supper. When he got back to his hotel that night he found that, for some mysterious reason, the packing cases had gone and somebody had evidently hosed down the concrete area. The water had turned to solid ice.

Sprog crouched with his back against the ventilator grille for a time, feeling dejected and resentful, as though somebody had deliberately robbed him of his bed out of spite. He peered at his new luminous watch; it was nearly midnight and suddenly, as if privately testing its accuracy, the chimes of Big Ben began to toll across the rooftops.

Sprog didn't fancy drifting off to find a different place to sleep and he didn't fancy a bed of ice, either. There were still plenty of packing cases down in the yard. Perhaps, if they weren't too heavy, he might drag one of them up the steps near the vent. Sprog had got rather attached to his vent.

It was worth a try. Sprog got up and, groping along

the dark wall, felt something catch the strap of his duffle bag. In the dim reflected light Sprog saw that it was a key — a key in the lock of the door. Somebody had been careless! Sprog turned it slowly, making sure that it didn't click too loud. Then he turned the handle and pushed.

He found himself looking down a steep, carpeted staircase lit by soft electric light. He heard no footsteps, no voices. His feet made little sound on the way down and, in any case, there was the enveloping murmur of the air conditioning plant.

At the foot of the stairs was a passageway leading to another closed door behind which came faint sounds of kitchen activity. There were other doors along one side of the passage. Sprog listened at the first, heard nothing and twisted the handle.

It was a small, unlit room giving off a smell of bleach and disinfectant. There were deep, wide shelves packed up to the ceiling with blankets, sheets and pillows. Sprog didn't stop to count his blessings, or admire his own enterprise. Without bothering to look for a light, he pulled the door closed and then, whipping off his shoes and top clothes, wriggled between the blankets and started out on the deepest, darkest, warmest kip he could ever remember.

The phantoms of the night got him within an hour. A switch clicked, harsh light seared into his brain and Sprog made out the forms of pale, astonished faces; a stout, indignant woman in a maid's uniform and a thin, important sounding man with a stiff toothbrush moustache and a uniform full of silver buttons ...

Sprog was still only half awake when he arrived at the

police station. He was interviewed in a room with a wooden table scattered with the crumbs of someone else's supper. The sergeant in charge had a heavy-eyed, weary, crumpled look as if he'd put his tunic on in his sleep and buttoned it up the wrong way.

"Right, let's sort you out." The policeman had a not very friendly, rather discontented manner — as if Sprog was a poor substitute for a major jewel robbery. He emptied Sprog's duffle bag, made him turn out his pockets and said, "Now, I've got a few questions and I want you to answer them. Truthfully, mind! What's your name for a start?"

"Sprog," said Sprog.

"Sprog *what*?"

"I haven't got another name," said Sprog.

"How old are you?"

"I dunno, exactly."

"Sprog," wrote the sergeant, mumbling the words to himself. "Age unknown . . . where do you live?"

"Birmingham," said Sprog.

"You're a long way from Birmingham."

"Yeah, well I'm on me holidays."

"What, on your tod?"

"I got lost," said Sprog.

The sergeant drew little rings with his ball pen, but he kept his eyes on Sprog. "You got lost," he repeated. "So you thought you'd spend the night at a posh hotel, even if it was only the laundry room."

"It wasn't much of a night," said Sprog.

"It isn't going to improve," said the sergeant, "unless you start telling me the truth."

He stood up with a massive, slightly menacing air and sifted for a second time through Sprog's belongings.

New clothes, old clothes; bits of left over food, a couple of comics, the torch. Brand new pocket knife, two halfpenny pieces, the golliwog key ring, scraps of this-and-that. The policeman gave everything a distasteful look, then his eyes moved to Sprog's wrist. "Where did you get that watch?"

"Bought it," said Sprog.

"What with — apple cores?"

"You don't think I nicked it?"

The sergeant sat down again. His face was more wakeful, a little sadder, but no friendlier. "Just a little kid, they said you were, at the hotel. I don't believe it. I reckon you're older than you look. And I reckon you've been in trouble before. You've absconded from somewhere."

"I never."

"You're a thief and a liar and stupid with it. Just because you're half-pint sized you don't fool me. You're old enough. Old enough to know better."

He fingered the canary coloured shirt, still in its plastic wrapping. He held up the jazzy tie, then he looked at Sprog's wrist again. Finally his eyes drifted back to Sprog's face.

"When I find out where you've come from and send you back, I'll see they throw the book at you. Quite a few quid's worth of stuff you've nicked here. You think you're quite a smart little tearaway, don't you? Well, you've had your fun. This is the end of the road."

"I'm hungry," said Sprog.

"In a minute," said the sergeant, scarcely softening, "you'll be asking for breakfast in bed."

He got up, though, went through a door and came back with a ham sandwich on a plate and a mug of steaming tea. He pushed these across to Sprog, who wolfed down the sandwich and nearly scalded his mouth with the tea. The policeman watched, waiting patiently until Sprog's mouth was empty. Then he drew the pad towards him and said, "Let's try again, shall we?"

"I never stole any stuff," said Sprog. "I earned the money."

"Where?"

"Washing down cars at a garage."

"Which garage?"

"Don't remember the name of it . . . it was near Piccadilly Circus."

The sergeant threw down his pen. "I'm not going to sit here all night listening to your fairy tales," he said. "You can go to bed, now. In the cells. Later on we're going to lean so hard on you you'll wish you were a stone wall, three feet thick. We've got a welfare officer on tap with a nose so long you could hang out washing on it. She weighs fourteen stone and she's used to dealing with kids like you. She'll find out all about you in ten minutes flat. She'll sniff it all out, all the way back to the day you were born."

Then Sprog knew, almost too late; he knew what he really wanted. "Hold on," he said. "I've still told you most of the truth. I didn't nick nothing, only . . . I have done a sort of a bolt. Daft, really. I dunno why I did it . . . I *have* got a home."

The policeman sat down again and clicked his pen. "Go on," he said, half believing. "Who with?"

"Me Uncle Bert," said Sprog. "I live with me Uncle Bert."

For a captured sparrow there was much at which to be

dismayed: to fly home, to be beckoned through an open window and fed from a firm, soft hand; to peck corn instead of crumbs, to be clipped and caged; to flutter away no more — a sparrow become a singing bird, an overfed canary!

As to whether all things would work out well, who should say? Who can count every barb, to every feather, of a sparrow?

But then . . . Sprog was not truly a sparrow. Sprog was Sprog — it had often been his proudest boast — but to *be* he would have, in the end, to *belong*.

The Boy, to be sure, had flown to freedom, driven out into the darkness where he had his own strange belonging — and how forlorn that last tilt of his white wings! But, for Sprog, the dark free night was left behind.

Thus Sprog sat in his cell, eating a second breakfast, watching grey light steal across the window bars — waiting for the Angels.